PRAISE FOR THE
Vera Kelly
SERIES

**2021 EDGAR AWARD,
G.P. PUTNAM'S SONS SUE GRAFTON
MEMORIAL AWARD WINNER**

**LAMBDA LITERARY
AWARDS FINALIST**

"Gripping, magnificently written . . .
a cool, strolling boulevardier of a book, worldly,
wry, unrushed but never slow, which casts its gaze
upon the middle of the last century and forces
us to consider how it might be failing us still."

—*THE NEW YORK TIMES BOOK REVIEW*

"Forget about 007. This heroine has her own brand of spycraft."

—*THE WASHINGTON POST*

"Knecht's novel is a slow-burn thriller, a complex treatment of queer identity, and an immersive period piece all rolled into one delectable page-turner."

—*ENTERTAINMENT WEEKLY*

"A splendid, genre-pushing thriller."

—*PEOPLE*

"Thanks to Rosalie Knecht's clever, hilarious writing, you'll find yourself wanting everyone you know to read it so that you can discuss together the wholly original, brilliantly subversive character that is Vera Kelly."

—*NYLON*

"Rosalie Knecht is an audacious talent, and her latest novel a propulsive, subversive gem. An intriguing mystery that will keep you guessing until the very end."

—LAUREN WILKINSON, author of *American Spy*

"With Vera Kelly, Rosalie Knecht has resurrected the detective novel for the 21st century. Sharp, self-possessed, and with a nuanced, meaningful knowledge of realities and histories well beyond her own, Kelly's take on who's lying and why makes for riveting reading in every scene."

—IDRA NOVEY, author of *Those Who Knew*

Published by Tin House, Portland, Oregon

Distributed by W. W. Norton & Company

Library of Congress Cataloging-in-Publication Data

Names: Knecht, Rosalie, author.
Title: Vera Kelly lost and found / Rosalie Knecht.
Description: Portland, Oregon : Tin House, [2022] |
    Series: Vera Kelly ; book 3
Identifiers: LCCN 2021062312 | ISBN 9781953534163 (paperback) |
    ISBN 9781953534248 (ebook)
Subjects: LCGFT: Novels.
Classification: LCC PS3611.N43 V474 2022 | DDC 813/.6—dc23
LC record available at https://lccn.loc.gov/2021062312

First US Edition 2022
Printed in the USA
Interior design by Jakob Vala

www.tinhouse.com

Vera Kelly
Lost and Found

ROSALIE KNECHT

 TIN HOUSE / Portland, Oregon

for Maëlle

APRIL 1971
BROOKLYN, NY

CHAPTER 1

Max liked to throw parties. The call would go out to the girls from the bar, the Harlem students who never went to Brooklyn except for her, and the confab of ladies we called *les grandes dames*, who lived in several apartments in a single building in Little Italy and spent their days making jam for each other and sending harassing letters to the editors of the *Village Voice*. The parties began with dinner. Max was utilitarian. She made vats of potato soup and bought loaves of bread from an Orthodox baker on Eastern Parkway, then appeared in a minidress and heels once the guests had arrived and fed the crowd like a camp cook, out of a giant ringing ladle. Afterward she put Sara Lee cakes on porcelain cake stands and set out a bowl of cigarettes. We would move the dining table out of the way, a collective heave, our shouting friends clenching their smokes between their teeth. They brought their own bottles. We supplied what we could. Max mixed sidecars and sours in coupe glasses for as long as it entertained her, then abandoned her post and came to dance with me. Our friends wove into corners together and reappeared, flushed; exes grew tearful and escaped to the stairs or the backyard. There were always a couple of girls asleep on cushions on the floor in the morning, and Max, who never woke with a headache in her life, made them coffee and eggs and sent them away with tokens for the train.

She had moved in with me in our first year together, after it had become plain that we were in love. I had been alarmed over it. Being in love had mostly been catastrophic for me in the past. I tried, being stupid, to give an impression of coolness, but Max wasn't fooled. "I don't think you like to live alone," she said. "Even if you say you do." She was living in a boarding-house on the Upper West Side at the time, and could have done with living more alone than that, since she had two roommates and washed up in a communal bathroom down the hall. It took only two or three trips in my car to bring over everything she had, and on the last of these trips, with her percolator and sew-ing machine balanced in the rearview mirror, we drove over the Manhattan Bridge just after the sun had set, the water of the harbor dark but still touched with red, Brooklyn glittering, and I understood that some journey had been concluded and I could rest.

She still worked at the Bracken, the bar in the Village where I had met her. I would go in sometimes and watch other women flirt with her, and then make a show of waiting for her at the end of the bar when she was finished, enjoying the envy of the room. I kept my office near Union Square, where I took private cases for investigation. It was mostly adultery and other emotional larcenies, but I'd also developed a specialty in

4

criminal matters that should have been the domain of the police, if the police had been willing to deal with people like us and we had been willing to deal with them. I collected evidence of embezzlement and fraud, bad checks, real estate scams that preyed on the owners of the theaters and galleries we all went to, and sometimes, once this evidence was assembled in file folders, my clients could force some action from the institutions involved. Sometimes not. It was hard work and often came to nothing. More to my liking was occasional freelance work I got through friends who worked in movies or television—mostly film editing, which I enjoyed for its absorption, the way I could go into an editing room and look up a while later and see that hours had passed. When I did well at splicing film together, a story cohered from the chaos of shots, and the better I did, the more the editing disappeared, leaving behind something sealed, smooth, holding itself together with an invisible tension, like a drop of water.

So the two of us kept irregular hours. Sometimes a day or two would go by when we didn't see each other, or we encountered each other only in bed at odd hours, as she finished her shifts, chatty but worn out from a long night, her feet and back aching. She would roll close and say, "My head is buzzing, help me sleep," her hands working under my clothes.

The house, which I'd bought with cash after coming back from the Argentina job in 1966, finally felt like it belonged to me. It had stopped being just a couple of narrow floors and their furnishings and had grown into something alive and particular, the way a house should. We had worked out where to put the chairs so they got the light in the afternoon, when we were most likely to be reading in them. We'd come across enough old prints and drawings to fill the walls. The pots and pans and implements in the kitchen had settled into natural locations. Max planted tulip bulbs in the backyard and was angry for hours when she realized rats had eaten them. She had to walk up to the Brooklyn Botanic Garden and soothe her feelings in the rose arcade.

I was thirty years old. The birthday had somehow come as a surprise. I had never been able to see very far into my future, and I didn't think about it much. I had lived since I was a teenager in a flexible present that extended not much past the first of the following month, when the bills were due. I think it was like that for a lot of us. The milestones that were required of women didn't really apply: I wasn't going to get married and I wasn't going to have a baby, and there was nothing else that was expected, so with each year I progressed a little further into an open expanse with no markers or boundaries, a kind of psychic heath. All I wanted for myself was money and Max, and maybe a dog someday.

Max disagreed with all this. She was twenty-nine. She said a person had to be heading toward something in order to live, but when pressed on what her personal ambitions were, she was evasive.

"I thought we had gotten over all those ideas?" I said. "The rat race and everything?"

"You can have ambitions that aren't a rat race."

This mystery held until I came in late one night and found all the lights on but Max nowhere around. I called her name a few times, but she didn't answer, and I climbed the stairs and found her in the second bedroom we had turned into an office, wearing the enormous headphones that made her look like a ship-to-shore operator, listening to Ravel on the hi-fi and making notes on a sheet of staff paper. That was how I learned she was writing an opera.

"All right, that's my ambition," I said. "My ambition is to support you in style while you write operas."

She covered her face with her hands.

"You're embarrassed!" I said.

"It is embarrassing. Don't make me talk about it."

She was a pianist with no piano. She had a secondhand Vox keyboard that she handled like a baby, though the wiring for some of the keys was beginning to go, and in order to get her hands on a real instrument she played on Sundays for a church in the Village that had a beautiful Steinway. She had played since she was a child and had that fixed, burning relationship with the instrument that made some people ruin their lives for music. She had studied in the music department at Vassar and had planned to go to a conservatory afterward. And then things had gone another way. Her family were the Los Angeles Comstocks, of Comstock Oil and Gas. She had been raised like a princess and then thrown out when she was twenty-two, after one of their private security men caught her on a vacation up the coast with her girlfriend. She had come back East and been a bartender ever since.

I wanted to give her a piano. I kept an eye on the classifieds. I had kept up this vigil for three years already, but hadn't managed it yet. Whenever I got a little money together, the house always needed it.

The girls around us were growing more placid as the years went by. One or two surprised us by going home to midwestern cities, marrying men and starting families. Those of us who remained vacationed together, going up to summer cabins in the Catskills. We learned how to row and fish. We guarded small pots of money for our unimaginable old age.

Some of us, it must be said, had gotten married too—a couple I knew had stood up on the steps of city hall with a pastor from the Church of the Beloved Disciple one afternoon in 1970 and took vows before news cameras, and were then cuffed and detained for blocking the public right-of-way. There were photos of them in their holding cells, flowers in their hair, holding up their ringed fingers to the bars. They were held for a couple of hours and let go. They still sometimes called each other wives when they were a few drinks in.

Winter that year had been long and cold, and we were so relieved when the first green buds opened in April 1971 that we went up to the mountains with a few friends for an early weekend. There was a cabin that we rented from an old farm couple, at the edge of a field patrolled by goats and a shrieking peacock. From the back steps, a sandy path led through ten minutes of woods to the shore of a tiny lake.

Max had been quiet as we packed in Brooklyn. She got that way sometimes, and I tried not to worry about it. She seemed preoccupied on the drive, said she had a headache, and didn't eat much when we stopped for lunch. We fought about this sometimes—she would disappear within herself and surface days later, confused about why I was upset with her. For my part, I couldn't admit to being upset, it made my skin crawl, so I shuffled around her rigid and quiet until the clouds dispersed.

Our friends Peach and Sylvia were already there when we arrived, unpacking cold cuts and cream cheese and smoked whitefish and cartons of pickles from the deli near their apartment. Sylvia built a fire in the pit in front of the cabin, and we had potatoes roasted in foil and sausages on sticks for dinner, as was our tradition, and then mixed drinks and carried them down the dark path to the edge of the lake. It was too cold to sit, but we sat there anyway. Max seemed more cheerful, and I allowed myself to relax, putting an arm around her, looking out across the black lake at the lights from a bed-and-breakfast and a row of summer houses on the other side.

But in the morning the mood had returned. I was too embarrassed to ask her about it in the cabin, where only a plank wall separated the two rooms from each other. The day was warm and bright, and the four of us decided to take the rowboats out to an island in the middle of the lake and see if we could have our breakfast there. Later in the season it would be too overgrown.

"But that's where I saw the snapping turtle," Sylvia said.

"You're afraid of an old turtle?" Peach said.

"You would be too if you had any sense."

This was the Peach and Sylvia vaudeville revue. Peach was from Staten Island and had such a limited understanding of the dangers of nature that she had once pushed a skunk out of the outdoor shower with a broom. Sylvia was from West Virginia and was forever chasing us out of patches of poison ivy where we were trying to have picnics. We packed the bagels and the deli things and some thermoses of coffee, filed down the path like a troop of Girl Scouts, and pushed off in the boat.

The lake wasn't deep and the water had the clarity of early spring. I could see straight down to the bottom, to schools of minnows darting over a field of silt. Green leaves opened on the surface, tethered by long umbilical stems. Far out over the water, birds dove through golden clouds of insects. "God, this is nice," Peach said to Sylvia, who was rowing.

"Why am I always the boatman on the river Styx?" she answered.

"I've got the way back," I said.

"She doesn't mean it," Peach said, looking at Sylvia fondly. "She likes to show off."

"Roll up my sleeves then, won't you, love?"

Max was looking around at the gauzy bright green of the hills. I would have pressed for her attention, but I didn't have anything in particular to say. She was working something out, I thought. Peach glanced at us once, scanned our faces, raised her eyebrows at me. I shrugged.

The island was a patch of earth held together by the roots of little trees a hundred yards from the shore. Sylvia pulled the boat up to it and Peach threw her arms around a leaning willow, and we stepped unsteadily ashore, almost losing the bag of breakfast things.

We spread a blanket, unpacked our food, and opened our thermoses. A trio of ducks fought and chased each other on the water.

"Is it romantic?" I said, nodding at them.

"What?" Max said.

10

"Whatever they're fighting over. Is it romantic?"

She was biting the rim of her coffee cup, her arms wrapped around her knees. I thought she wasn't going to answer me, and I was already beginning to feel the suffocating warmth that I always felt when I was angry or dismayed but knew it was too trivial to say anything about. But she said, "Isn't it always?"

I took that as encouragement. "Are you all right?" I said. Peach and Sylvia were picking their way back toward the boat for insect repellent, and we were more or less alone.

She pushed her hair out of her face and inspected the sky. I waited.

"I got a letter from my sister," she said.

⊕

What did I know about the Comstocks in April 1971? I had known a few things before I ever met Max. I knew of the Comstock Institute, the premier educator of petroleum engineers in the United States, and by happenstance the alma mater of my mother's father, who had inspected rigs in Louisiana and Texas. I knew of the Comstock Collection, one of the largest privately held art collections in the world. I knew that Comstocks appeared often in the politics of the West—state senators, commissioners, chairmen of infinite boards.

And I knew a little about how Max had been raised. She talked about a house in Los Angeles and a ranch in San Luis Obispo. I could sense that words like "house" and "ranch" were euphemisms, in a family like that, for immense ecosystems of people and property. I had tried once or twice to get at this point—a misguided desire, I guess, to emphasize that I was the unlanded one of the pair of us, even though I had grown up in a plush and well-connected neighborhood outside Washington, DC, myself, and even though Max had been completely dispossessed at twenty-two.

"How big is the place in Los Angeles?" I had said. "How many rooms?"

And Max had said, "How many *rooms?*" in a way that made me understand not only that there were very many rooms but also that I hadn't chosen the right measure. Another time she said, "I used to walk down to our post office—"

"Your post office?"

"At the ranch, yeah. It was my job to walk down to our post office twice a week and get the mail. If Dad had letters, he would drive down, but he always made us kids walk. It was a big thing to him, to make us tough. My brothers loved it."

"You had your own post office?"

She had laughed. "Things are bigger out west," she said. "We were our own town."

She told me that when she was a little girl in Los Angeles, she could see the Comstock oil derricks from her nursery window, their great heads bobbing in the blue haze. I knew all that. I knew that Aimee Semple McPherson once came to the house, in Max's grandfather's day, to ask for money to build the Angelus Temple. "He talked about it for the rest of his life," Max said. "Because she didn't ask, she sort of commanded him, which people didn't often do. And he said she wore sequins in the daytime."

But that was all. She had told me very little, in three years together. The subject of her family was painful, and her silence sometimes made her seem to me like an émigré from a small and distant country that no longer existed.

⊕

"They're getting divorced," Max said.

"Your parents?"

"That's what Inez said."

I could hear Peach and Sylvia splashing in the water on the other side of the island.

"Is this the first time anybody's written?" I said. "Since you left?"

"No, not the first. Benny wrote me once right after it happened and called me a lot of nasty names and said I was killing our mother." Her older brother, the firstborn. "And Inez writes sometimes at Christmas. She's the only one I sent my new address to when I moved in with you." Inez was the youngest of the three Comstock children. "Inez is sweet, but she's not tough. I think she would have liked to be nicer to me, but it would have made them mad."

"So what did Inez say?"

"That Dad and Amma are getting divorced." She looked at me, embarrassed. "That's what us kids called them."

"Amma?"

"Benny called our mother that when he was wee. So now Amma is living in the Park Royal Hotel in La Jolla and Papa is holed up at the Los Angeles house with—I can't really follow what Inez is saying. She's too sweet to say unkind things, but then she doesn't end up saying much at all. It sounds like there's a woman living there with him. And some friends of the woman."

"Oh, no."

She drew in a shaky breath. "Why should I care at all, Vera? Why should I care at all?" Her eyes reddened, but she didn't cry.

"Well, but you do," I said, putting my arm around her.

"I don't," she said. "I just remember everything." She stared at the water. "Inez wants me to go out there."

"She does? What for?"

"The walls are falling in, you know? She thinks if we were all there . . ." She shrugged.

"They certainly left you out when they felt like it." I was agitated in her defense.

"Yeah, of course they did."

"So why should you go now?"

"Who said I was going?" she said.

I relaxed.

"I wish I could explain it to you," she said. "I could talk for days and I couldn't get it to make any sense."

"I might understand it," I said.

"There's too much," she said. "Forget my family. Who can even understand Los Angeles?"

⊕

I thought it was settled. Maybe my mistake was in trying to extrapolate from my own family, which was so small, just my mother and me, and my mother was a redoubtable woman who would never call on me for any kind of assistance, in any circumstances. I had no brothers or sisters, and my father died when I was twelve. I was a disappointment to my mother, and when I was a teenager she was harsh and obtuse with me. We didn't speak much now, and I didn't worry about her. Probably no one had ever worried much about Elizabeth Kelly. She once got in a wreck in our old Studebaker and arrived home in a taxi with three stitches in her forehead and all her dry cleaning, which she had made the driver stop to pick up on the way home from the hospital. She would not be dissuaded from an errand and she was not interested in the opinions of other people and she had never misspent a dollar in her life. It was a mystery to her why I couldn't master my life the way she had mastered hers.

Max slept badly when we came back from the mountains, and over the course of a few days she became distracted and irritable again. One night I got up for a glass of water at three in the morning and found the kitchen door open a crack, and cigarette smoke wafting in from the tiny backyard. Max hardly ever smoked.

"Sweetheart?" I said into the dark.

"Ah, hey," she said.

I came out onto the step. The sky was yellow overhead, but it was hard to make out her expression. She was sitting curled up in the Adirondack chair in her work clothes, her hair unpinned.

"What are you doing?" I said. "You just got home?"

"A little bit ago. I had a good night, took a cab."

"Spendy baby."

"Don't scold."

"I'm teasing. You know I don't like you on the train this late anyway." I sat. "It's chilly out here. Come to bed?"

"I'm not tired yet." She looked tired.

"Who'd you bum that cigarette off of?" I had quit the year before. The smell made me nostalgic for a lot of wasted time.

"A new girl at the bar. She was getting in my way all night."

"Then it's the least she could do."

"That's what I thought."

We listened to a siren coming down Flatbush Avenue. "Inez wrote again," Max said.

I took that in, examining my feet.

"He's going to marry the new woman," Max said.

"God, that fast?"

"Amma's all alone in some hotel." She rubbed the back of her hand across her eyes. "What if I did go?" she said.

Somehow I was relieved. All the tension of the past week had been an effort to avoid this, and here it was. She could do this and then we could get back to normal. "What if you did?" I said.

"Would you think it was stupid?"

"I would think it was family."

She smiled. An airplane droned low overhead, a red-eye bound for LaGuardia.

"Will you come with me?" she said.

I hadn't expected that. "Won't they—"

"Yeah, yes. But I—" I think she wanted to say, *I can't do it by myself*. But that wasn't the kind of thing she said. "They might be awful about it. You don't have to. I would understand."

"Of course I will," I said. I glowed.

She reached across the gap between us and squeezed my arm. After a minute she said, "You're in for a ride."

⊕

16

I could take a week off, I thought, without doing too much damage to the couple of cases I had. One was a young woman looking for the father of her daughter, who owed her a great deal of money and had told her he was going to pick up shifts for a while unloading cargo on the docks in Bayonne, but could not be found. Another was an older gentleman of my acquaintance whose landlord had been trying to get his rent-controlled apartment out of his grip. Construction had been going on in the units above and beside his for months, and I was fairly sure, after a few weeks of observation, that it was unpermitted and out of code, and that there were times when the only worker there was a rangy kid banging at random on the walls and floor with a hammer. I gave all parties my answering service and assured them that I would be able to wrap up work when I returned. We would fly out on Monday, April 26.

"Is that your opera?" I said to Max. There was an old shirt box on the bed, the lid not quite on, and I could see a stack of papers in a binder clip inside. I had found her packing in our bedroom, very slowly. She would take a dress out of the closet, smooth it out on the bed, fold it, and then stand looking at it for a while.

She put the lid on. "It's a copy of the draft," she said. "It's not done."

"You're taking it along?"

"I thought I might get a chance to see my old piano teacher," she said. "While we're out there."

It stung, briefly, that she would show it to someone else when she hid it so carefully from me. But then, I couldn't read music.

17

"Who are we going to tell your family I am?" I said. I had been thinking about this every day.

"They'll guess," Max said. Now she was digging absently in the box of costume jewelry she kept on her dresser. "They know all about me."

"I suppose so."

"That'll be the least of their concerns, I think," she said.

CHAPTER 2

As a kid I'd had the dreams of California that everybody has. I had a subscription to *Photoplay*. My father used to take me to movies on Saturday afternoons when it rained. He was a serious man but he liked comedies, and we saw *Adam's Rib* together, and *Singin' in the Rain*, and *His Girl Friday*, which he loved so much we saw it twice—he was a newspaperman, after all. We sometimes stopped for lunch on the way home, and we would sit at the counter with cups of coffee—mine half-filled with milk—and read books. He was capable of a pleasant and comfortable silence that I rarely encountered after he was gone. My mother's silences were tense, and the silences of my girlfriends always made me think I had done something wrong. I suppose I was the one who lost the knack, actually, for being with other people quietly. I had been trying to teach it to myself again since Max moved in.

My idea of California had been planted by Busby Berkeley and tended by advertisements for cars and cigarettes, so I felt both a deep estrangement and a giddy sense of recognition as the plane banked over arid mountains and began its descent into LAX. There were the palm trees down the avenues: a perfect match for themselves. Max was waking from a restive nap. Turbulence boiled up from the hills, and I clutched her arm, but it was more from excitement than fear.

"It's just air," she said, laying her hand over mine.

I wanted to point it all out, but it was ordinary to her, or worse. I tried to imagine what it would be like for this scene, the gauzy endless city beside the shock of the blue Pacific, to be freighted with homecoming feelings. Maybe she felt nothing looking down but the regressed irritation that I always felt when my train pulled into Union Station in Washington. We were low enough now to allow each palm tree its own spiky shadow. Cars shone like beetles on the exhausted gray of looping freeways. The wheels touched down, rattling the drink carts in the galley. Max exhaled. I looked for the mountains, but they were gone. "Smog," she said.

We collected our luggage and stepped out through glass doors to the sidewalk that faced the air traffic control tower, which looked like it was from space, a fairground disk looped with superfluous buttresses. This semidesert light was new to me. I had traveled, but mostly to places that ranged from damp and cold to damp and hot. Here the sky was distant and immobile. Some beautiful young women in minidresses were arranged like the Three Graces around a pay phone, having a drawling argument with someone who had failed to send a car. A man in a half-unbuttoned shirt and gleaming shoes was tranquilly smoking a joint in the taxi line. I wished I hadn't buried my sunglasses in the bottom of my suitcase.

"Should we get in the line?" I said. "How far is it? I brought a lot of cash just in case."

Max was chewing her lip. "Well," she said. "We could. Or."

"Or?" I waved away a redcap. "Oh—they'll send someone?"

"They might have already sent someone."

I saw where she was looking. In the middle lane of traffic, there was a long cream-colored car with a chrome grill like the Lincoln Memorial. It merged right and came to a gentle stop in front of us, the windows tinted, the driver invisible, a winged woman poised to leap from the hood.

"Max," I said. "This is for us? This is a Rolls-Royce."

She didn't move. The driver's side door opened, and a man in a gray suit and cap took the long walk around the front of the car.

"Hey, Maxie," he said. "Long time."

"Chuck," she said. To my surprise, I saw she was trying not to cry. It was like watching watercolor wick through paper. She hugged him. "I figured you retired."

"I got a few more years in me." He patted her twice and they separated.

"Vera, this is Chuck," Max said. "He's been driving for my family for—I don't know."

"Twenty-three years," Chuck supplied.

"This is my friend from New York," Max said, and I shook Chuck's hand. He smiled, took our two valises, opened the trunk. The lie was nothing. It evaporated before it touched the ground.

We drove through white sunlight, over baking concrete, and into a raw zone of oil derricks. This seemed like too much—that the lines connecting the woman beside me and this city would appear so quickly and be so visible. It was impossible to see the massive, slow activity of the pumps as anything but animal-like, a flock of long-legged, heavy-headed prehistoric birds at work in the soil. I looked at Max bug-eyed.

"They're ugly, aren't they?" she said.

"Are they?" I said. "I don't know."

We left them behind and entered an ordinary mess of department stores and supermarkets and movie theaters, framed against lunar hills and fronted with date palms. The smoked glass of the car windows colored the world tan. I sat neatly and anxiously on the seats, which were cream leather. Max sprawled instead, as if she were in a beat-up taxi at home. "There's hardly anybody out," I said.

"There are people," Max said. "You're used to New York." Then, as if thinking this might have sounded like a rebuke, she added, "When I first came back East, I couldn't believe how crowded the streets were. It felt like every day was the Thanksgiving Day parade. I used to have to take two deep breaths before I left the boardinghouse."

"Where are we going?"

"Bel Air."

"How far is that?"

"Ten or fifteen miles. Chuck, how long did it take you today?"

"Forty minutes."

"Not bad," she said.

I had worn one of my best dresses. The embarrassing thing was that I had lost sleep over the question of what to wear. I knew enough about these things to wonder if it was wise to try to impress at all. Wasn't that always the fatal mistake of outsiders?

But then there was the other fear, always present at moments like this, of appearing unfeminine by underdressing. I chastised myself for this fear—so many of our friends wouldn't have cared, or would have called me a sellout for caring—but there it was. The Comstocks would assume, probably, that we were together, no matter what Max chose to say, and the idea of presenting myself to such people looking like a cartoon of a Wellesley lesbian, with undone hair, in slacks—I couldn't handle it. In the morning I had watched Max style her hair and put on one of the dresses she reserved for playing the piano on Sundays, and with relief I followed her lead. Now I was left only with the question of whether my dress, which was from Penney's, looked cheap. I hoped not. It was a good fabric. But how hopelessly petit bourgeois, to think about fabric.

Stucco apartment complexes flashed by, their names in looping script. The lack of sleep was catching up with me, and my eyes were heavy. I tried to nap, my head propped on my fist, but it was precarious. When I opened my eyes again, the car was approaching a broad white gate, along a median planted with Mesozoic vegetation.

"This is the house?" I said, startled.

"This is Bel Air," Max said. "East Gate." Her face was set. Her posture was careless, but I could see she was pulling on strands of her hair.

"Are you all right?" I said.

"It's just been a long time," she said.

Inside the gates it was quiet and green. Max rolled down her window, and we felt the breeze that stirred the eucalyptus leaves. White mansions appeared on the hillsides. Tall hedges, immaculately cut, edged the road. Here and there, a break in the trees revealed a gatehouse, a driveway, a fountain. We passed an English manor house, set on grass that was trimmed as close as the felt on a pool table. Ranks of sprinklers ticked and waved.

"It's like a movie," I said, then wished I had thought of something cleverer.

"They're all the same," she said shortly. "All these houses. They all want to tell you where they got the stone."

My parents had been house-proud. Neither of them had had very much growing up, and they had made good. We had a tidy brick three-bedroom on a street lined with old trees in Chevy Chase, Maryland. By the time I was fourteen or fifteen, I had begun to grasp what it all meant—the street, the schools, the tennis club, the music lessons, the barns out in Montgomery County that advertised boarding for horses, the murmur of petition arising from Methodist churches on Sunday mornings. All my friends' mothers had a good front room where they hosted visitors, and beside the coffee table in each of those front rooms was a magazine rack filled with issues of *Architectural Digest* and *Better Homes and Gardens*. At Christmas we drove to neighborhoods even luckier than ours to process slowly past their crèches and North Poles. On very special days, the little girls of Chevy Chase were taken to tea at the Mayflower Hotel, where they could watch senators' wives entertain diplomats' wives. We aspired; it was virtuous to aspire. We aspired to what I was seeing here through the window of the Rolls, if we could imagine it. I wanted to say all this, but of course Max already knew it. The truly rich, they knew what we wanted, didn't they? And what could they do from up there but avert their eyes?

I had been to the Aurora a few times, the boardinghouse where Max lived for four years before she moved in with me. I'd lived in places like it myself for a few bleak stretches before I was recruited by the CIA. There were rats in the walls, and the cold leaked in around the window frames. Ginny old nurses lived on the fifth floor, teenagers from the Midwest on the second, trying their luck, sometimes getting turned out by bad boyfriends. A house full of secretaries and waitresses and widows living on sardines and day-old bread. Girdles drying on clotheslines in the air shaft, coffee scorching on hot plates.

"Did you ever feel sorry for yourself?" I said to her. "When you were on your own? I mean, if you were used to this."

"No," she said.

I wondered if that could be true.

"When we were little, we had a nanny who told us every day that we were the luckiest children in the world," she said. "She would say it when she put us to bed at night. 'Remember that you're the luckiest little children in the whole world.'"

We turned onto a narrower street that wound up a hill.

"It was such a big house," she said. "Sometimes we couldn't find anybody at all."

The car slowed at another gate, this one cascading with wisteria, a name in ironwork script across the span: IL REFUGIO. Another man in a gray uniform stepped out of a booth and opened it, waving the Rolls through. Ahead I could see a driveway switchbacking up the side of the hill, and above us, in the full glare of the midafternoon, attended by its own sprinklers, a castle.

Silence reigned in the car. Finally Max said, "My grandparents built it. My grandmother had a particular sensibility."

"It's crenellated," I said. It gripped the hill like a perching raptor, gray stone, feathered with ivy, with a facade that could have held off a siege. Its defensive pose was undermined by a network of open terraces that clambered down the slope in front, ringed and connected by pergolas and arcades of white columns, by shrubbery, by fountains with spewing gods—I squinted: Were they all Bacchus? Pointed towers rose here and there. I counted three immense balconies and a stained glass rose window over the front door.

"She was from Oklahoma," Max said. "She's dead now."

"Oh, it's, I mean—" I searched for words.

"Chuck, can you let us out here?" Max said, leaning forward. "We'll walk up."

"Of course," he said.

I got out and went around to the trunk to get our bags, and then realized that it was, in a place like this, an insane thing to do. Max had gotten out and was standing on the fine gravel, her arms crossed, lost in private thoughts, unencumbered even by her purse. Chuck left us and I watched the gleaming car turn left, flicker through a grape arbor, and then disappear into a large, white-painted horse barn. In the distance, out of the hush, there was a scream. I flinched and stared around.

"Ah," Max said. "The aviary."

"Max," I said, catching my breath, "is there anything I should know, any—any hints, anything, that would make this easier—I mean, what do they expect from people?"

"There really isn't anything," Max said. "I wouldn't know where to start."

"Is that a *drawbridge?*"

"It's ornamental. They filled in the moat." She brushed off her skirt and started up the hill. "I'm so hungry," she said. "I hope they kept something from lunch."

CHAPTER 3

The front doors were opened by an invisible hand. "There's a camera," Max said. "They can operate the door from the staff office upstairs." We stepped through into an immense stone hall like the nave of a church. I looked up: the ceilings were painted with horses, an elephant, ancient soldiers with push-broom helmets. Hannibal crossing the Alps? A tiny woman approached out of the gloom.

"Miss Comstock?" she said as she got closer. She was gray-haired and tidy, not in uniform, slightly out of breath. "Your sister said you would be coming. It's lovely to meet you. I'm Mrs. Woods, the house manager since three years back." She had stopped fifteen feet away, next to a wooden statue on a plinth of Saint George treading on the neck of the dragon. The figure towered above her, luridly painted and much abused, as if it had been dragged behind a car. Her hands were clasped; a bracelet on one wrist was trembling. "We've set up a guest cottage for you. Is there anything at all I can get you right now?"

"Thank you so much," Max said. "I'd like to see my father, I think."

"Mr. Comstock is very busy this afternoon," Mrs. Woods said.

A silence rolled around the great room like a dime in a carnival game. "Is he?" Max said.

"He is," Mrs. Woods breathed.

"That's surprising," Max said. "Busy where?"

"He is—he doesn't like to be interrupted—"

"Oh, doesn't he?" Who was this merciless person? I looked sideways at her. I had once watched her eat a plate of cod in a restaurant when she had ordered a chopped steak. She never pushed people, really. She lost interest in her own minor wants as soon as they inconvenienced anyone. "Is he in his study?"

"I couldn't say, miss."

"Right." Max turned to me. "It's not far," she said. She walked past Mrs. Woods. I followed her. "Which cottage?" she asked over her shoulder.

"Delphi," said Mrs. Woods.

"So kind of you," Max said. "We'll be sure to let you know if we need anything."

I followed her up the stairs, onto the second-floor gallery, and down a hall mosaicked with scenes from some classical arcadia: nymphs swimming in rivers, gold tiles glinting in their hair. Tall windows looked out over the hills. Below us, beside a little pool, a woman sunbathed nude with a magazine. "Is that your sister?" I said.

Max stopped to look. "No, I don't know who that is," she said grimly. She turned toward a half-open door. "This is Amma's sitting room," she said.

I glanced in. A profusion of modular furniture in pale leather marked off sections of a huge room. At the far end, centered before windows, was a marble statue of a draped woman balancing a water jug on her hip.

"Was her sitting room," Max said. "I suppose."

"You really don't think she'll come back?" I said.

"Aloysius doesn't change his mind," she said. "And anyway, how could she stand it even if he did? The humiliation."

Wisteria waved through the windows. I thought Max might walk in, but she didn't.

"She was always so proud of that statue," she said. "She haggled it away from some abbess in France. Her hairdresser put a wig on it once and she thought it was the funniest thing in the world."

We took a turn up a short flight of stairs, and Max knocked on a carved door. "His study," she said.

I wrung my hands beside her. "Are you—prepared?" I said, thinking of all the years gone by.

She pushed the door open. "Dad?"

It was a wood-paneled room, the walls hung with murky paintings, and there was a set of french doors open to the implacable California sun. The largest painting, ten feet high, depicted a man on horseback. Its style was neoclassical, with billowing fabric and Greek light, but the man was dressed like a cowboy—or a wildcatter, I thought, seeing the tiny oil derricks distinct in the bottom left, and recognizing now that the vague landscape painted allegorically behind and around him, at fractional scale, was the San Gabriel range.

Through the french doors, a balcony offered a view of dark oaks climbing a distant slope and, far off, the blue line of the

Pacific rounding off the world. A television played to the empty room. There was a sound from the balcony, the click of a glass being set down.

"Inez?" Max said.

A woman appeared at the french doors, squinting amiably into the dim interior, shielding her face from the glare with a newspaper. She wore a bikini and a sheer dressing gown; her hair was pinned up, and the smell of suntan lotion rolled off her. She was about twenty-five and looked like she was made of velveteen.

"Oh my goodness," she said. "Are you Max?" She rustled and clinked toward us and then put out a single hand and brushed Max's sleeve with the tips of her fingers, as if she wanted to embrace her but hesitated lest she offend. Her face was aglow. "I'm *so* glad to finally meet you. What a blessing this is."

Max couldn't find the words. I could see her thinking *Who are you?* and fearing the worst.

I interceded. "This is Max," I said.

That roused her. "And this is Vera," Max said. "You are—"

"God, I didn't say, did I?" She laughed. "I'm Callisto." She clasped Max's hand.

Max's mouth kept opening and closing. I thought she was trying to find some way of saying *Are you the woman?* But she was failing at that, we both were. Instead she said, "Where's my father?"

"Oh!" Callisto said. "He's exercising!" She pointed to the balcony and we went out. Below, on a tennis court, was Aloysius Comstock. He was shirtless, white-haired, and very tan, and he was standing on the red clay court with a couple of free weights at his feet. Off to one side, on a folding chair under a beach umbrella, was another man. He was dressed in a summer suit and was reading a paperback through the kind of goggle-like sunglasses a bomber pilot would wear.

"Who is that?" Max said. The question was becoming baleful. I could hear it echoing all around the house, unsettling the comfortable strangers who were roosting there.

"That's St. James," said Callisto. "He and your dad have become such good friends."

⊕

Max and I had a late lunch in a dining room with a painting of the Annunciation on the ceiling. We scraped our cutlery and ground our pepper beneath the rolling eyes of the angel Gabriel. On a sideboard, a Sterno hissed under a chafing dish of salmon. Periodically Mrs. Woods appeared, always coming from the far side of the long room, so we watched her approach as if we were meeting her in the arrivals hall of an airport. Each time she surveyed our plates and added something to the phalanx of condiments on the table. On her last visit, accompanied by a younger woman who cleared the plates, she said, "Mr. Comstock has invited you to dinner."

She left. I looked closely at Max while she sat next to me, drinking the coffee that had come at the end of the meal. I felt that I was being led by a guide who had forgotten our shared language. Her hair was done the way she did it at the bar—loose, but pinned back from her face. The windows in this room were high in the wall, as if to confound an invading force. I couldn't understand the way the house was put together. Its parts barely communicated with each other. Upstairs were the airy Greek spaces, down here the cramped medieval. I couldn't form any question about all of this that would do anything but highlight the galactic distance that existed between her childhood and mine. Such questions would make me look dumbfounded and flat-footed as well, which I hated more than anything. So I sat quietly and watched her stare up at the unreachable windows.

"I'm so tired," she said.

"When is dinner?" I said. "She didn't say."

"It's always at eight," she said. "Let's go lie down."

"Where's our luggage?"

"It'll be in the guesthouse already."

The guesthouse Delphi was white and terra-cotta, set on a marble terrace at the lip of another swimming pool, this one quite small, with a row of discreet orange trees shielding it from the winding driveway. In a little topiary prison, a nude plaster milkmaid fed grapes to a leering goat. The inside of the swimming pool was tiled in a shade of Aegean blue that, in spite of everything, in spite of the smutty statuary and the muddled hulk of the house and the flaying sun, brought up some old and confused thrill in my heart, the part of me that could not get over Maxfield Parrish, even when I knew better. There was just so much light and air and space. The ocean silent in the distance. Max looked at none of it, bumping through the front door of the house with an irritated shove of her hip, making a wall of bougainvillea shudder. "I thought they would give us this one," she said. "It's the farthest away."

We found her valise immediately, in a bedroom with a gold ceiling and heavy curtains around the bed, as if a dynastic couple might need to consummate a marriage there with their retinue gathered around. My suitcase wasn't there. It took a short search to turn it up in a smaller bedroom, next to an uncurtained bed, with a view of the wilder and emptier side of the hill.

"Your friend from New York," I said, and she looked a little shamefaced, then annoyed.

"You need Chuck to know?" she said.

"I don't need anything," I answered, and as I said it a wave of dismay came over me, because I recognized the state I had just entered: too tired, too far from home, becoming a child. Perhaps, even worse, becoming a sixteen-year-old again. Making claims that weren't worth what you'd pay for them.

"It's just easier," she said.

"You said your family knows anyway."

"That's different from saying it," she said.

We stood looking at my suitcase. The sound of trickling water drifted in from the pool.

"It is, yeah," I said.

"If we were in Washington," Max said, flushed now, "what would you say to your mother?"

I couldn't imagine. I pictured Elizabeth Kelly, reading the *Post* in the sunroom and eating melba toast. I had wondered sometimes about her and my father and what their romance was like in the beginning. They were so reserved with each other when I was a child, so rarely in the same room. I hadn't been able to square their behavior with the idea of a wedding at all, the pledges of devotion, the biblical poetry, the expectation of kissing and dancing together in front of people. And then he died. If I turned up in her parlor now with Max, a person

35

about whom I would gladly make any pledges suggested, and whom I still couldn't embrace after three years without pausing to breathe in the smell of her soap—it would all be too much, completely embarrassing, her daughter not just a lesbian but a soppy one.

"I know, I know," I said, picking up the suitcase and heading back toward the big bedroom. "Forget it. You should nap. You hardly slept last night."

I watched her maneuver into the curtained bed. It was fascinating to stand in this hysterical fantasyland and watch a person be unsurprised by all of it. Not a glance upward at the carved ceiling, not a moment for the deranged rococo fireplace, which was ringed with putti heads in black marble and gold. I left her there and found the kitchen—normal, though huge. There was coffee in the cabinets and a quart of fresh milk in the refrigerator. I made a pot and then walked from room to room, being astonished in privacy. In a drawing room, there were framed photographs on the wall of a movie actress from the 1920s, whose name I couldn't quite remember—studio headshots, an alabaster face surfacing from chiaroscuro, a net of diamonds in her hair. And then a snap of her in an evening gown and stole beside a pool, which I recognized after a moment as the pool in front of the house I stood in. Her head was thrown back and she was laughing, her pose with the fur a little campy, as if to say, *Can you believe it, little old me?* I found my way out of the back of the house and sat on a bench under a trellis of wisteria. A dusty cat appeared, and I watched it stalk a lizard, pounce, and miss.

⊕

Max slept for a long time. I lay on a lounge chair beside the pool, reading, and then the sun and the smell of heated earth knocked me out too. I woke sometime later, itching with a light sunburn, to see a woman climbing the steps up to the terrace. She was out of breath, her hair swinging in a secretarial bob, wearing a sundress splotched with flowers. She had Max's freckles and round chin.

"Inez?" I said.

"Yes!" she said. "Yes." She came over and shook my hand.

"I'm Vera," I said, wishing I had gotten up from the lounge chair first.

She let go of my hand and backed away. "Max said that she was bringing you." She looked around, saw nowhere to sit, and remained standing.

Max had said that Inez was twenty-six, but her manner was nervous and expectant, as if a surprise party might break out at any moment, and she seemed younger. She had a husband and two children; hard to imagine, although now that she was standing close I could see fatigue around her eyes.

"Glad you could come," she said.

I thought that probably she wasn't, but also that she didn't want me to feel bad about it. "Max is sleeping," I said, but just then the door opened behind us and Max stepped out, her hair undone, her makeup rubbed away.

Inez squealed and darted at her. I watched them hug; Inez rocked her sister back and forth. "Well, hello," Max said. Were there tears in her eyes? It had been seven years. She turned aside, trying to re-pin her hair.

Inez didn't want to let go of her arm. "Chuck picked you up?" she said. "I called the airline for the arrival time. Did you eat already? Why did they put you out here? Olympus is empty too, a bunch of awful people just left. Have you been swimming? Is it dusty in there? Mrs. Woods only started to air it out yesterday. God, I've been here for a week, Max, I'm going to lose my mind. You have to meet the kids. They're napping now, but tomorrow. They're happy, anyway. Did you see there are goats? Dad got a herd of goats, I can't even tell you, he's doing the most ridiculous things—he advertised in the paper for a goatherd. And he got seven applicants, driving up here with their tongues hanging out, you can imagine. But the kids love them. If I let them, they would sit in the pen all day. They stink!"

"Goats?" Max said.

"And a cow! An Indian cow. You have to see it, it doesn't look like an ordinary cow at all." Inez hugged her again and then looked her over. "You're thin. I like your dress."

"Did you come to prepare us for dinner?" Max said.

"Prepare you? You don't have to change. Dad's pretending to be informal now."

"No, I meant . . ." Max trailed off. "We met Callisto."

Inez's face grew somber. "Max, she's younger than I am."

Max pressed her hands across her eyes. "Is he really—?"

"She's twenty-three. She was a theater student at UC Davis. You should see her room—things everywhere. All over the floor. It's like the kids' playroom. She sleeps until eleven in the morning."

"And he's going to marry her," Max said.

"That's what he says. Amma's blood pressure is terrible. She has Grandmother with her in La Jolla. And the dogs." The two of them sat down on the top step. Inez kept squeezing Max's hand. I could picture them as little girls, Max leading every charge, Inez chattering behind. Max looked dazed. Her hair was red in the light, which was turning toward evening. The morning seemed like it had happened weeks ago—the two of us packing our bags upstairs, me still irresolute over which shoes to bring, Max checking and rechecking the back door and the burners on the stove.

"He told her two months ago he wanted a divorce," Inez said. "They were playing tennis! Can you believe that? Amma said they hadn't played tennis in months and then one day he wanted to play and afterward he said, 'I want a divorce.' And she was just shocked. Shocked. She said the earth opened up."

"Just out of nowhere?"

"Oh, I don't know, Maxie. You know how they are. How they've been. But however they've been, they've been that way a long time. She told him to pray about it. She had her minister come to the house and have lunch with him. To no avail. And everyone told her she should be patient, so she tried—she told me in a letter that Dad was sick, which I didn't understand! I guess she meant that he wasn't himself. She thought he was having a nervous breakdown. And then one day a car rolled up with Callisto in it, and he said she would be staying here."

"They were already—?"

Inez waved that away. "I don't even want to think about it, how long it might have been going on. He'd been going to these soirees at the Fairfax place, I think he met her there. Mr. Fairfax is a filthy old man."

"And Mrs. Fairfax has been zonked for fifteen years."

"She never sees anybody but her astrologer. You could run a circus through her house and she wouldn't notice."

"Who are all these *people*?" Max said. "We saw somebody naked by the pool, for God's sake."

"Can I smoke?" Inez said. "I'm dying for a smoke. I don't do it in front of the kids." She turned around, remembering I was there. "I'm sorry, Vera, do you mind?"

"Not at all."

She extracted a pack from some hidden pocket and lit one. "I don't know who they are," she said finally. "That's the part that worries me, to tell you the truth. Dad says they're his friends. Friends from where? Have you met St. James?"

"No. We saw him, though. With Dad."

"I don't know how long he's been here. Dad says he's not living here, but it's obvious he is. Every time I see him, he's coming out the front door of Dodona. Dad says he's a writer. I said, 'What's he written?' And Dad said, 'Thousands of things.'"

"Oh, no," Max said.

"They're always together," Inez said. "They sit up late talking. I have to admit, I asked Mrs. Woods what the guesthouse looks like inside. She said it's tidy. Which was a surprise. And she didn't want to say anything else, she takes her work very seriously, but I could see she thought something was strange and then she said, 'He has quite a lot of incense, I always open the windows.'"

"Well, that doesn't mean anything. Just some kind of hippie."

"He's got to be fifty years old if he's a day. I talked to Em too. She's the chambermaid on the weekends. She says he brought his own food. He has a dozen jars lined up on the counter in the Dodona kitchen with powders and herbs and twiggy things."

"Tea?"

"I don't know. He gives me the creeps, Max. He wears necklaces. Roger thinks he's a queer."

You're never prepared and it's always one step away. I looked somewhere else. I could see Max stiffen and draw her arms in.

"No, Max, I don't mean anything," Inez said. "That's just what he said."

"I know, it's fine."

Inez glanced back at me, failed to find anything to say.

Max said, "Well, how did he end up here in the first place?"

"He's a friend of Callisto's. Or she's a friend of his. And there are more. There were nine or ten of them staying in Olympus all last week. I kept the kids away from there. They all seemed high. They had a fire every night. Not inside. Behind the house, in a pit." She finished her cigarette. "Look, I'm glad that Dad invited you to dinner. I think that's a good sign. It makes me so sad, you know? That you've been gone."

Max said nothing.

"But listen, Callisto and St. James and whoever else, they'll be there too," Inez said. "They've been at dinner every night. So honestly, if I were you, I'd have a drink first. Roger can't stand it, he eats early with the kids." She put her arm around Max again and then stood and brushed off the back of her skirt. "I have to get back. I'm playing hooky. See you at eight. It'll be in the solarium." She turned and waved at me. "Nice to meet you."

⊕

At seven thirty, while I combed my hair and chose something fresher to wear, I tried to confer with Max. "Is your brother going to be there too?"

"He was supposed to fly in tomorrow, but something came up. He's coming next week. Inez is upset, she wanted us all here at once."

"What is dinner usually like?"

She paused. "Well, usually my mother is there," she said, and then laughed. "And usually it's a long time ago."

CHAPTER 4

The glass walls of the solarium extended from the back of the house. It glowed alone on the darkened lawn, like a ferry mid-crossing. We could see the dining table as we approached, a uniformed woman standing by a sideboard covered with bottles, and a tame forest of potted trees that circled the room, their leaves lit from below by candles and lamps. No one else was there. We were the first to arrive. Max paused outside and took two deep breaths. The night was dry and eddies of sage drifted around us. She looked at me and squeezed both my shoulders and then hugged me.

"Jesus," she said.

"It'll be all right," I said. "All they can do is be horrible. And who cares?"

"They could be horrible to you."

"Isn't that what I came for?" I said. I was relieved to be leaned on. I would fight them all off. I would turn over the dining table and carry her away. They would never know what hit them. I was nervous.

"They're all going to be late," Max said. "Let's go in."

The maid seated us. "I'm Elaine, if you need anything," she said. "Will you have a drink?"

"Cognac," Max said. "In honor of Grandmama." She smiled at Elaine. "She drank coffee and cognac. She had it chilled on hot days."

We sat together on one side of the table. I felt blinded and vulnerable, surrounded by dark windows made opaque by the lamplight, hemmed in by trees, like a child at a campfire in a deep wood. Music began to play, faint strings. Elaine said, "Mr. Comstock likes to have Vivaldi at dinner."

"This is all Amma's," Max said to me. "She's good with plants. She used to invite the horticulturalists in from UC Santa Barbara and take notes."

Inez appeared from the door that led into the house, her face newly pinkened with blush and lipstick. She was bright-eyed all over again to see her sister. I wondered sometimes if things would have been easier growing up if I hadn't been an only child. There was no other point for navigation. Just my parents and their chilly intrigues, their laden silences. And then a cavernous grief that was strictly the property of my mother, like everything else in the house. I didn't know how a child was supposed to grieve, and no one told me.

"They're always late," Inez said happily, sitting down across from us. "Elaine, could I have a whiskey sour with a couple of cherries?"

"The trees are beautiful," I said. Lemons and figs, and something I didn't recognize with a silver trunk and high, knotted roots. Bushes with glossy dark leaves and white flowers. The room was fragrant. It was a good wine that I was drinking. This kind of thing made me see the point of money.

"Do you remember Grandmama's cognac?" Max said to Inez.

"All day!" Inez said.

"Oh, only at the end. When we were kids, she was very scrupulous about five o'clock."

"I miss her," Inez said. "Just the other day I was trying to tell the kids that story about the dance and the horses, and I couldn't remember how it went."

"The dance where she met Grandpa?"

"Right, and her horse was lame."

"The horse was lame," Max said, "and Grandpa drove her and her sisters home, and she didn't want him to because it was so far and they were so poor and she didn't want him to see the house. But he thought she was trying to stop him because she didn't like him. So then he was too shy to come back and visit until she sent her little brother to thank him with a jar of gooseberry jam."

Inez glowed with satisfaction. "I knew you would remember it."

"We all heard it a thousand times."

Inez said to me, "Our grandmother was supposed to be the prettiest girl in Oklahoma."

Max said, "They were so poor they had no shoes."

It had an incantatory quality. Was this just something Americans did? I was thinking of the painted ceilings. We liked them so much better if they vaulted over the head of a person who had gone barefoot as a child.

"Do you live in Los Angeles, Inez?" I said.

"We live in San Diego," she said. "Me and Roger and the kids." She was looking at Max again. Her face was sharp with pain. "You haven't seen our place. I keep forgetting. When we moved in, I would talk to you sometimes about it! Just by myself. So I felt like you were there."

Max was stiff in her chair. "Inez," she said.

Elaine stepped into view with the bottle of wine I was drinking from, wrapped in a towel, and refilled my glass.

"Inez, none of it was my decision," she said.

"But you didn't try," Inez said. "You didn't try to come back. Not even for the wedding."

"I wasn't invited to the wedding," Max said.

"You didn't try," Inez said again.

Max leaned across the table and put her hand on Inez's, which was small and white, a child's hand, set with a jagged diamond. "Dolly, I don't think you really understand. The way things were for you here—they were never like that for me."

The door opened and Aloysius Comstock walked in. Max and Inez got to their feet, as if pulled by strings, and I stood up too, clumsy with my chair. He was, as we had seen from the balcony, very tan, and he was wearing an orange shirt. As he stepped into the room, he adjusted the heavy watch on his wrist and touched his hair, as if trying to project casual ease to the back row of a Broadway theater. Inez crossed the room and kissed him on the cheek. Max remained standing but didn't move. I knew immediately that Aloysius wouldn't be the first to speak.

"Hi, Dad," Max said.

He regarded her silently. I thought I might levitate out of my shoes. Elaine stopped halfway across the room, holding a drink she had already made for him. Three or four seconds ticked by.

"You brought a guest," he said.

This was a masterful move; none of us had expected it. A burning spotlight shone on me. Max said, "This is Vera."

"Nice to meet you," I said. High tension sometimes made me brassy; I gave him a little wave.

"Vera is Max's friend from New York," Inez said.

He assessed me, head to toe, and then silently turned to Elaine, releasing her from her spell. She put the drink in his hand, and he came to the head of the table and sat down.

"I don't want to fight," Max offered.

Inez said, "She just got in this afternoon. Mrs. Woods put her in Delphi."

"Inez tells me you're a bartender," Aloysius said.

"Yeah," Max said.

"Yes," said Aloysius.

"Yes," Max said, stiffening. "I'm a bartender."

"Uncle Robert was a bartender after he got out of the navy," Inez said, as if this exculpatory idea had just occurred to her.

Elaine said, "Are we waiting for another guest, sir?"

"Two more."

Elaine retreated to the sideboard. Max said, "We met Callisto this afternoon."

Aloysius smiled, as if he couldn't help it. But it passed quickly. "Good. Yes, she said. She thought she surprised you."

Inez strained with things unsaid, like a balloon inflating.

"How did you meet her?" Max said.

"At a performance," Aloysius said. "Of new music."

Callisto herself came in from the house door then, wearing a short cotton dress that drifted around her, a little rumpled. She looked like she had just picked it up off the floor and put it on in a hurry. When she approached the light of the lamps, I saw that she was flushed, her hair sweaty at the temples, which made me think that might have been exactly what had happened. That the two of them had just been in bed and had spaced out their entrance to dinner in this unconvincing fashion. I glanced at Aloysius, who was busy with his drink.

"Sorry I'm late, everyone!" she sang out, and sat down to Aloysius's right.

"One more, sir?" said Elaine.

"Yes, Elaine. Didn't I say?"

St. James came in through the far door. We all looked up. He wore a hat with a brim, a black thing that called to mind a Spanish priest. He offered it to Elaine as he came in, and she took it with a gesture that either was ironic or could not help but look ironic. Her face was very set. St. James glanced around at us amiably. "Late again," he sighed. "The coyotes are hunting."

"Been consorting with them?" Aloysius said, and then startled us all with a loud laugh, which St. James joined in.

"Too old for consorting!" he said. "I have to just stand and listen." He accepted a drink and sat at the foot of the table. An ancient rule of etiquette surfaced in my brain, stamped all over with my mother: it should have been Callisto at the foot, if they were engaged. St. James had a rubbery English accent, bending oddly around his vowels. A long time in California, maybe. He was pale and had a long face with unexpectedly open, childlike eyes. It was hard to figure his age—his skin had a waxy quality. He might have been fifty or sixty. His hair was gray but thick. As Inez had said, he wore necklaces. As I looked him over, he settled his hands on the table, smiled to himself, and then abruptly met my gaze. I studied the lemon trees, feeling caught out.

"St. James, this is my older daughter, Maxine," Aloysius said.

"Lovely to meet you, Maxine," said St. James, raising his glass.

"And you," she said. I tried to see her the way he would. She didn't smile as she raised her own glass, but she left the impression that she had. Inez's feverish attention to Max gave her place at the table a certain magnetic pull. Aloysius's coolness did as well. I was seated closest to St. James, and I could see that the pendant on his gold chain was a saint's medal. Not so scandalous. I wondered if Inez had recognized it as such. Were there many Catholics in these hills? I doubted it.

"This is my friend Vera," Max said, and she squeezed my hand under the table.

"Vera!" St. James said. "What a name—a great name. Faith. Are your people Russian?"

"No, not Russian," I said, taken aback by his warmth. "My mother's family is Irish. My father was half Armenian."

"And the other half?" He had the manner of a person drawing out a shy child on the first day of school.

"Irish as well," I said. "Kelly."

"Black Irish," he said.

"I don't know, I think that's the Armenian," I said, touching my hair. It was dark and curly, and I got quite a tan in the summer. I had these puzzled conversations with people every so often, about where all that had come from.

49

"The black Irish, you know," St. James said, addressing the table, "are descended from Spanish pirates. Love children of poor homesick boys from Galicia and Asturias. Can you imagine? Kidnapped onto ships and forced to raid sheep farmers. All that rain."

"Where are you from, St. James?" said Max.

"Regrettably, I'm English," he said. "I come from Devon."

"Regrettably?" said Inez, not quite loudly enough to make anyone respond.

"I've heard Devon is beautiful," Max said. "And Cornwall."

"It's the real, old England," Aloysius said.

St. James accepted this praise with an inclined head. "Arthur's country. But stifling."

"And you're a writer," Max said.

"Also regrettable, also true."

Elaine brought out salads on a cart. I was relieved to have something to look at.

"Aloysius," said St. James, "I was taking a look at that little piece of property today. It's beautiful. Covered with poppies. Purple thistles down at the bottom. And the air is so lovely." He paused and closed his eyes before continuing. "Very good air."

"It'll do, then, you think?"

"I'm troubled by the drainage."

"The drainage? But it hardly ever rains," said Aloysius.

"But when it does! It must just pool there at the bottom of the slope."

"I haven't seen it happen."

"We Englishmen," St. James said apologetically, turning to the women, "we think of rain."

"Are you building something?" said Max.

Aloysius glanced at her but did not respond.

"An educational center," St. James said.

"Who are you planning to educate?" Max said.

"All are welcome," said St. James.

"It has to do with the goats," Inez said carefully.

"Higher ecology," said St. James.

Callisto was clutching a fluted glass of seltzer. "Agriculture is part of it."

"Agriculture," said St. James. "We husband ourselves."

"I'm sorry?" Max said, blinking. I exercised heroic control over my face.

"As a species," St. James said. "We become stewards of our own kind, as one more species among many."

"Is the cow involved as well?" Max said.

Aloysius said, "It'll be a world center for ecology and agricultural research. I've been speaking to the governor."

"Daddy has had some meetings," Inez said. "He went up to Sacramento."

"That sounds quite expensive," Max said. Aloysius looked up sharply.

"God," St. James said, puffing out his cheeks. "I suppose it does."

"Inez," said Aloysius, as if this conversation were not happening, "have you finished the kitchen?"

"Almost," Inez said. To Max and me she said, "We're redoing our kitchen in San Diego. We have to get out of town every weekend just to keep from losing our minds. It's a disaster zone. We've been going to our place up the coast so we can cook eggs in peace."

51

"Ah," I said, and then, searching for something to say, "a renovation." That was inadequate. "What a nightmare."

"Vera has her own house," Max said suddenly. "In Brooklyn."

The eyes of the table turned to me. "The roof has been driving me crazy," I ventured. "I keep getting leaks. I think it's squirrels."

"You have to poison them," said Aloysius.

"Oh," I said, as if this were a directive I'd just received by telegram. "Well, I've just been trying to find the hole they're getting in through. I've been up there four or five times with a flashlight, in the crawl space—"

"Once they find a way in, they keep finding it," Aloysius said. "We have a man who comes in with strychnine."

"That doesn't sound very ecological," Max said.

"Predation is a part of ecology," said St. James.

"Boy howdy," said Max. "Isn't it just."

"Ecology is a system of energy passing from one living being to another," St. James said. "Up and down chains, and outward from individuals to clans, species, kingdoms."

There was a brief silence. Elaine refilled the glasses. A waiter who looked like a high school student cleared away our salad plates and distributed tureens of something dark in a cream sauce.

"But that's not the same, is it?" said Max. "Dad's not eating the squirrels."

Inez intervened. "The cow is really a pretty thing," she said, "and so peculiar. What kind is she, St. James?"

"She is a Sahiwal," said St. James.

"She has a hump," Inez said. "And her ears droop down like a dog. Like a beagle! She's that color too."

"They're the best milkers in India," St. James said. "And beautiful. People hang garlands of flowers around their necks."

"How long have you been staying in Bel Air, St. James?" said Max.

Aloysius looked again at his daughter. He was angry. I suspected that he was organized by anger, that his prodigious energy derived from it. It was his parents who had made the money. What does that leave a person to do? To wait as things drift into his hands. To train with weights and develop philosophies. Max had said that he painted. I could believe that. Large canvases, I guessed.

St. James said, "I come and go. Sometimes my work takes me up the coast."

"You talk as though you live here," said Aloysius to Max.

"Me?" she said.

"Are you concerned about the use of this home, Maxine?" said Aloysius.

Max set down her soup spoon. I could see pink spreading up the back of her neck. "It's just that my mother used to live here," she said. "And now Callisto and St. James do."

If I'd had a knife on me, I would have reached for it then. It was like the moment in a Western when someone is accused of cheating at cards. Max sat perfectly still in a little blaze of fury.

"*Max*," said Inez.

"You used to live here," Aloysius said. "And then you were no longer welcome. And yet here you are. With this person." He looked at me. Elaine came through the door from the house, saw this, and backed up against the wall. "I can't imagine why you would bring this person here unless you intended to be thrown out. It's disgusting. You should be glad your mother isn't here. What would she think?"

"I know what she would think," Max said.

"She would wonder how she could have gone so wrong with you. Look at you. Are you proud of yourself?"

St. James had risen from his chair and was coming around the side of the table. "Please," he said, and his voice had dropped a register, "she's a very young person, Aloysius, and she's suffering."

Max stood up from the table. "You sent me away and I went away," she said. "That was the best thing you ever did for me."

Inez was crying.

"Max, let's go," I said.

"I don't want any part of it anyway," Max said. "I don't know why I came."

"You came because you thought you could worm your way back in," Aloysius said. "You came because you're tired of this obscene little game you've been playing."

"Let's *go*," I said again.

"I came for Inez," Max said. "You can rot. This man is scamming you and you deserve it."

She walked toward the outside door and I ran after her. Inez's voice had risen to a wail. I saw St. James's face last: he had managed somehow to come up with an expression of gentle grief, like Christ in an El Greco painting.

CHAPTER 5

Max flitted ahead of me in the dark, too angry to slow down. The breeze was heavy with Pacific scents I didn't recognize. I worried I would break my ankle on the slope, or she would. A swimming pool, lit like a jewel, shimmered and undulated beneath a sky that was colored campfire orange. I could see the lights of other estates, and down the canyons, over the flanks of other hills, the glitter of ordinary city streets. From up here, it was difficult to imagine the parking lots and shopping centers we had passed that afternoon.

"Wait up!" I called. "Come on, baby."

She stopped and bent her head forward, her fists clenched. I caught up to her and held her shoulders, trying to see her face, but she kept turning away. "What was I thinking?" she said. "You know my plan before was to never speak to him again, and I really meant that, I was never going to see this place again until he was dead, and maybe not even then." She sat on the ground. We were in an odd part of the estate, a forgotten patch where the grass was sparse, near a utilitarian outbuilding that was screened from genteel eyes by a stand of trees. "He said horrible things to me when they caught me with my girlfriend."

"I'm sorry, love," I said. I sat beside her.

"Not just angry things," she said. She took half a breath and seemed unsure how to finish it. "Disgusting things about— about women. Being with women. It was—my mother was embarrassed by me, and she wanted me to marry this boy they liked and the whole thing—that was my job, I was the oldest girl, and she was upset because her plans were ruined and she was angry, and maybe I can understand that, in a way. But my father—I don't understand it, he was so revolted, and he said such revolting things, that made me feel—I just wanted to tear my own skin off. It took weeks for that feeling to go away. I would have burned this place to the ground if somebody had given me a match." Her hands were flitting in the air. I put my arm around her waist.

"I don't think we should be here," I said.

She put her head in her hands. In the woods, a series of short yips became a howl. I started. From the direction of the main house came an answering fusillade of barks, and then a male voice cursing. "Guard dogs," Max said, lifting her face. "German shepherds. Or they used to be. They must have a whole new crop of them now."

"There's not a thing here that I've ever seen before in my life," I said. "It was a coyote, wasn't it? That howled? It's the Wild West."

"Bel Air? It's something else." She laid her cheek on her knees. "It's a planet with a very thin atmosphere."

I pictured her at the bar, the pretty turn of her wrist as she filled a glass, charming the shy girls who came straight from Midtown offices in the afternoons, and later, her calm even as the dancing and carousing reached a crescendo on the floor; working, listening, leaning close to hear orders, and with all this behind her, trailing into the dark.

"We'll pack up and go," I said, already thinking about whether it would be difficult to change our return tickets, or too expensive. Maybe we would have to hole up in a hotel somewhere for a few days and go back on Saturday, when we'd planned to. That wouldn't be so bad—I was cheering up, thinking about it, preparing to say something to Max. We could go to Venice Beach. We could lie around all day and eat ice cream by a hotel pool. It would be more than we had planned to spend, but circumstances were conspiring. We could go to the Santa Monica Pier and play rigged games and get sunburned. See her old piano teacher, sure. "Max, we'll just—"

"He's such an obvious con," Max said.

"St. James?" I said.

"I thought my father was more sophisticated than that. I really did. Since we were tiny kids, they were always telling us to watch out for that kind of person, you know? If you're a family like us—a family like this . . . people are always circling."

"It doesn't matter, Max."

"He's so oily."

"We'll go to a hotel. Make a nice vacation of it and never see him again."

There were tears in her eyes. Suddenly she was irritated. "It's hard. My sister."

"Right, of course. I know." I was contrite.

"She was always the favorite. Well, no. My brother was Aloysius's favorite. But she always ran after him, trying to please him. And my mother always treated her like a doll." She pressed the heels of her hands into her eyes and breathed deeply. "I spent so much time minding her out at the ranch, just the two of us." She sat up. "I wonder if my Avanti is still here. It was in my name." She got to her feet.

"Where are you going?"

"I just want to look in the garage. It was a nice car."

"It can wait, can't it?" There was a hazy quality to her face, her gestures. She marched down the slope. I scrambled after her.

"It was my car," she said.

Her general coolness and reserve were interrupted sometimes by moments like this, and maybe because they were so rare, it was almost impossible to divert her from them once they had begun. When she first moved in, I sometimes chided her about her clothes, her cleanliness—she left things everywhere. She had been dismissive and flippant about it, so I hadn't realized the criticism upset her until it was too late. One morning, I had brought a pile of her discarded clothes down the stairs and dropped them in the living room, exasperated because she hadn't put them in the hamper. She was sitting on the sofa drinking coffee and, as I learned later, recovering from a bad night at the bar—shorthanded on a Saturday night, running out of bottles, exhausted, just missing a train home. She looked at the pile of clothes on the floor and then set her coffee cup down on the end table, stood up, and walked straight out of the house. She was wearing slippers. I ran out to the stoop, remonstrating with her to come back in, but she didn't even turn. She was gone for an hour and a half, and by the time she came back I had come to understand a thing or two about myself and had taken the pile of dresses and underthings back upstairs. She could laugh about it by then and called me an idiot. Her slippers were filthy. She had sat in the park until she could see straight again.

I chased her down the hill in the dark. I couldn't tell where she was headed, and she was too far ahead of me to ask. I realized as we dropped onto the smooth shelf of the driveway that she was going toward the horse barn where Chuck had parked the Rolls that afternoon. Just above the barn, on another white terrace, was another guesthouse the size of a village church. It was whitewashed, which gave it an ascetic quality, even with its own pool in the terrace and its own yew hedge and objectionable statuary, the exact nature of which I could not make out in the dark. I was suddenly confident that this was Dodona, where St. James reigned. Max was ahead of me, opening the garage doors. I hurried through the grape arbor, hissing, "Wait." By the time I got to the open doors, she was inside, invisible, a series of footsteps and soft thumps.

"They don't keep it locked?" I said. My breath was coming fast. I was uneasy, thinking of the dogs. We belonged here but did not belong here. We were allowed but not allowed. Her father frightened me.

"Not this early. They lock it up on rounds after ten." A click, and the huge room was filled with icy light. Max stood at the far wall, pleased with herself. Between us stretched row after row of gleaming cars. Closest to me, there was a Jaguar in racing green, and I put out my hand and palmed the snarling hood ornament.

The cars were in perfect ranks, as if they had been squared up with a ruler. It smelled like cold concrete and gasoline.

"There it is," Max said.

Farthest in the back, all the way at the end of the row, in shadow under the haymow, was a silver-blue sports car. Max stood looking at it. I picked my way across to her. "They only made them for a year or two," Max said. "Amma bought it for me." She sounded sad. "When I turned twenty. I wanted to take it back to Vassar with me, but then Chuck explained about the salt on the roads. So I left it here."

She wanted the car back and was embarrassed about it. It was cleaner to want none of this. "It's pretty," I said. It was small and its lines were smooth, with tense curves, suggesting the containment of power.

She glanced at me. "It was nicer than my brother's car," she said, and smiled. "He always got the best of everything. But my mother had her little subterfuges." She walked to the car and I followed her. The soft top was up. The paint shone. It looked like it had never been touched by human hands. She opened the driver's side door with a loving twist of the handle. "The keys are in it," she said.

It was at this point that I looked up and saw St. James standing in the darkness just outside the open doors. We hadn't been gone from dinner long; had it broken up in our wake? He was still hatless. His hands were clasped behind him.

"Max," I said. She was sitting in the driver's seat, one foot still on the concrete, running her hand over the dash.

"I wonder if anyone drives it," she said.

"Max."

She looked up, and then climbed out of the car. St. James advanced into the garage and stopped at the first line of cars, in the full glare of the overhead lights. He looked older here, his hair disheveled rather than wild.

"What do you want?" Max said. She was holding the car keys in her hand, and she seemed too aware of them, as if they were evidence that she'd been interrupted in the middle of a felony.

"I saw the lights on," he said. "Perhaps I should go get your father."

Max turned pink. "Excuse me?"

St. James didn't repeat himself.

"This is her car," I said.

"Who the fuck," said Max, "do you think you are?"

Her eyes were wide. I put my hand on her arm. She didn't acknowledge it.

"I've met plenty like you before," Max said. Her neck was mottled white.

"I could say the same," St. James said.

"You talk a lot but you're just a pimp," Max said. "There are hordes like you in this city."

If he was surprised to be spoken to this way, he hid it well. I tightened my fingers on Max's arm, but I could see that she was rapidly moving out of my reach, out of her own reach.

"He's a filthy old man," Max said. "And you're a parasite."

St. James waited for her to stop. He smiled and relaxed into contrapposto. He said, "You know, Maxine, before you came, I spent months here. And nobody ever mentioned you at all." He took a few steps forward and let his hand rest on the hood of a red coupe. "I thought Aloysius had one daughter."

Max's hands were shaking.

"St. James," I said, "please go."

"I don't care what you do," Max said. "His money doesn't matter to me. But my mother has rights, and she'll see what's happening here. I wouldn't stick around if I were you."

"I never even saw a photograph," St. James said, with a shrug, and then he withdrew, his footsteps on the asphalt fading away.

When he was gone, Max sat down in the driver's seat and cried. I walked around to the passenger side and let myself in. We sat together in the shadow of the soft top and she sobbed on the steering wheel.

"It's just nerves," she said finally. "I've been ringing like a bell since we got off the plane."

"It doesn't matter what he says," I said.

"No, he's right," she said. "I knew it anyway. Ask me in an hour and I'll tell you I don't care."

She was up late that night. She seemed tired of talking, and I was so worn out that I fell asleep in the big bed without digging my toothbrush out of my suitcase, with all the lights still on. I woke disoriented a few hours later, as Max was turning out the lights and climbing in beside me. I rolled over and murmured a few words to her. She had been distant and abstracted all week, and we hadn't had sex. This caused me a shuffling, embarrassed anxiety, a feeling of being an urchin tapping at a window. The day we'd had, the alien country, had made it worse. I put my arms around her, moved as close as I could, felt what she was wearing—a nightshirt, which I pushed up. She responded at first, but then seemed to drift away.

"Are you all right?" I whispered, as if we could be overheard.

"I'm just tired," she said. "Don't stop."

She finished and I fell asleep, reassured. When I woke in the morning, she was gone.

CHAPTER 6

At first, of course, I thought she must be somewhere nearby. Her suitcase lay open on the floor where she had left it, with folded clothes toppling out. I washed up and brushed my teeth and dressed before I began to look for her. The kitchen of the guesthouse was bright and empty. A coffee mug sat alone on the shining plain of the counter. I wondered whether breakfast was served in the echoing feudal hall where we had eaten our reheated lunch the previous afternoon—were regular meals set out, like in a hotel? I mentally chided Max for not leaving me a note, and then thought I was rushing to judge, that she was probably out on the terrace in the sun. I looked in the refrigerator for something to eat, enjoying the anticipation of walking out and seeing her there in one of the deck chairs, her casual posture, the way she treated this fantastically rarefied and costly environment as if it were a railroad apartment in Queens. There was nothing at all in the refrigerator but milk and white wine. I walked out to the terrace. Max wasn't there.

I was uncertain. Il Refugio made me feel like Max and I were, at best, tethered to each other in space, like astronauts. I didn't know what to do without her, even though I scolded myself for it. I usually thought of myself as a fairly clever and adaptable person, someone who could find her way around a new place without a map. I trailed landlords through the Bronx for a living, and regularly fielded threatening letters from other people's husbands and bondsmen and lawyers. And yet I was completely unmoored here. I stood on the steps where Inez had huffed up to speak to us the day before, looking down on the world. When I found Max, I decided, I would press my point about going to a hotel. This was too much. It wasn't doing either of us any good. I felt so lonely here, even when I was standing right next to her. And the only way I could understand her quiet and remove was to guess that she was suffocating. That the effort to survive the presence of her father took all her concentration.

I hesitated a long time before going to the main house, hoping she would appear, walking up the dusty slope or tumbling down from the woods. I entertained the notion that she had gone to get breakfast and would bring it back. As the sun climbed, I had to admit that this was probably not the case, and I went to get my shoes, resentment in my heart. How much time passed while I dithered around the guesthouse, feeling slighted? Was it an hour? Ninety minutes? The sun lashed the hill. The smell of sage carried up from the canyons in waves. I started out, then went back to get my sunglasses.

By this time it was nearly ten. Hawks circled. From somewhere downslope, I heard a bell tinkling; I wondered if it was the herd of goats that had been so much discussed. I was practicing what to say when I found Max: *Leave no man behind.* I approached the main house, feeling like an insect, looking in vain for an insect-sized entry among its colonnades and trellises. I went in the front door instead and crossed the monumental, empty entrance hall. I wished for Mrs. Woods. The place felt haunted by Aloysius, as if he were a spiteful shade already instead of the thriving, living owner. It was the unsettled way he moved, the way our eyes helplessly followed him around a room. I had no idea what I would say to him if we came upon each other here. I registered, with surprise, the fact that I hated him. I rarely hated anyone and had known him such a short time. I chose a hall that I hoped was the same one that had taken us to the dining room the day before and started down it, past a relentless farrago of tapestries. It was clear that he also hated me. But his hatred of me preceded my actual arrival in his home. His hatred of me had been hypothetical before I appeared and made it specific.

I was lucky: here was the dining room, with its display of coats of arms, its defensive disposition of windows. There were no chafing dishes on the sideboard. A single chair was out of line, at an angle to the table. I had missed breakfast, then. Max had said the place was so big that sometimes, as children, they couldn't find anybody. I felt how possible that was. I wasn't just alone: other people were dangerously out of reach, as when you are crossing a desert at night and your car overheats. But that was dramatic of me. I left the room and continued down the hall, thinking that sooner or later I would have to come to a kitchen, and a kitchen would have cooks in it. There was a lump of real anger in my chest by now. Max had to have known how hard it would be to find her. Why not leave me a note? Why not wait for me?

I got to the end of the hall and found no kitchen. How far did they make the staff walk with their scalding platters in this place? I went on. At the foot of a set of stairs I thought I heard a voice in an upper room, but when I stopped to listen, there was nothing. The house itself did not tick or creak. Sometimes a draft stirred around my feet, an emissary from the distant out-doors. After another turn, there was a brown-painted door set in the wall—at ordinary scale, which made it jarring, in this house where everything towered. A gold stencil said SERVICE. I knocked twice, got no answer, and pushed through.

Here was the kitchen, or a kitchen. A woman in a white apron was running a torrent of water into a pot sink from a wide-open tap, her back turned to little Mrs. Woods, who was shouting over the noise. Elaine was flouring a worktable. They stopped and turned when I came in, except the woman at the sink. Mrs. Woods's face was open, irritated, the face she didn't show to guests. Elaine recognized me, and I saw her eyes widen in panic. Without knowing why, I felt the first contracting tug of dismay.

"Good morning," I said. "Have you seen Maxine?"

Something was wrong. I could see Mrs. Woods's mental scramble. Elaine went to a cabinet, kept her back to me.

"Good morning," Mrs. Woods said. The woman at the sink turned off the faucet. In the quiet, something in a pan crackled in fat. "You would like breakfast?"

"No, thank you," I said slowly. "I'm looking for Maxine."

Mrs. Woods paused minutely. "I'll go and see if I can find her. Could you wait in my office?" She pointed to a door at the far side of the room.

"That's all right," I said. I didn't want to wait at all, or be enclosed. But I didn't want to argue with Mrs. Woods either. "I can stay here," I said, but of course that wouldn't work. The entire point of a house like this was to keep people like me out of the kitchen.

"I'm afraid it's very busy in here," Mrs. Woods said, and she was accessing some inner authority now, had found her footing. Elaine dropped a lid, which revolved on its noisy edge. "Elaine will bring you some coffee." Mrs. Woods opened the door to the office and stood aside. I did as I was told. It was a small room with a window into a rosebush; the desk was cluttered and there was a visitor's chair with a pile of invoices on it, which Mrs. Woods removed. I sat down and Mrs. Woods smiled at me and shut the door.

There must have been some horrendous fight already this morning. Some scene. I ran my fingernails back and forth over the arms of the chair. How bad could it have been, to be causing this paralysis of embarrassment? Had Max managed to find something shocking to do? Had she broken a window? Knocked Callisto out with a vase? I should find Inez, I thought. She would tell me what had happened. Everyone else here was only an extension of Aloysius. But I didn't know where she was staying, in a guesthouse or here in the main building.

Elaine came in with the coffee, set it on the desk, and backed out. I left it there. I scanned the papers I could see from where I was sitting. Household business: delivery slips for beef and eggs, a work order for landscaping. My mind jumped here and there. Being trained the way I was, I gathered a lot of useless information out of habit that would never yield anything important at all, stray threads that connected to nothing. You cast a wide net into the sea and bring up bottles and tin cans. Most of what I learned from everyday observation was the grimy stuff of life that did no one any good to know: soured love affairs, addictions, small cruelties, sadnesses half-hidden under indifference. Max was also an observer, by nature although not by training. She was curious about my former life in the CIA and teased me about it sometimes. I had been in infiltration as well as surveillance. She had an idea that it had been glamorous, and I had tried to explain that it was mostly transcription, the boredom broken up by precipitous and insincere friendships made under false names. It was corrosive, and only my own incompetence saved me from doing more harm. Recently, Max and I had gone to a rally against the Vietnam War in Union Square, and I held back anxiously, keeping to the sidewalk. Some of the speakers talked about the CIA, its secret influences around the world, its conspiracies, the butchery in Indonesia, the secret bombing of Cambodia. They had a ragged and excited air, a kind of agitated certainty. On the train afterward, Max said, "Some of that stuff was a little wild, right?" and I said, surprised, "No, they were right." I hadn't been privy to active projects outside my own, of course—I was a field operative, a front-liner, very low in the hierarchy. But I had lived inside the logic of the organization for those years, and I knew what it thought of itself and how it saw its place in the world. My venture in Argentina had been so small in the grand scheme of the agency, and it was its very smallness, afterward, that shocked me. That the agency was willing to toy with ordinary lives so far away, on such a flimsy basis, and with such a bored, patient, limitless expenditure of resources—to crush, or try to crush, a few students with heated nationalist ideas that, in the end, my handlers had barely understood. It was a minor farce, the cartoon at intermission between the bloodshed in the Dominican Republic in 1965 and the escalating carnage in Vietnam. It was difficult to explain my shame about this period to Max. It was too exotic.

I thought then, sitting in Mrs. Woods's office, giving in finally and drinking the coffee, that maybe I had kept too many things private from Max, even as I was frustrated by her reserve. There were days when a complicated silence hardened between us, and I moved around the edges of it, unsure whether I had put it there or she had. Once we were watching an old Western on TV in which a cattle thief rode across a desert, and a long shot from the air showed him alone on his horse in infinite, arid solitude, and Max, standing up from the sofa to go to the bathroom, had said, "That's you." I had laughed, but it rankled. When she came back, I said, "Who are you, then?" and she said, "I'm the horse."

"So we're together, then," I said.

"Well, yes," she said, "but we don't speak, and you're sitting on me."

I must have looked upset.

"It's a *joke*, sweets," she said.

"Freud says there's no such thing as a joke," I said.

"Well, no one ever claimed he was any fun."

I teetered between insisting on ruining a joke and guarding my private worries, and as I always did, I chose my private worries. Did she have them too? She had made comments, from time to time—jokes, again—about how I made more money than she did, and owned the house, and that she was a burden or a kept woman. I joined in these jokes, because that was our silent agreement, and told her that if I was paying the light bill, then she should put on something pretty for dinner, and that kind of thing. She was funny about money. I had always been patient in that area, knowing what I did of her upbringing, but now, being in this place, I thought I had probably not been patient enough. She was miserly over small things. She had the zeal of the converted and often listed prices out loud. If I sent her to the grocery store alone, she would come back with dented white-label cans, dehydrated potatoes, whatever fruit was on sale because it would turn by the afternoon. We had a fight once because I hired someone to clear out a drain, and when she heard how much it cost, she said I should have tried harder to clear it myself.

I had been waiting twenty minutes. I was restless. I kept thinking of Elaine's face. Something was knocking around in the back of my mind, and I was trying to ignore it. Some unease. Of course, it would take twenty minutes to get anywhere in this house, I thought.

Surely Mrs. Woods had better things to do than personally fetch Max? How would she know where she was, anyway?

I got up and went back into the kitchen. The woman at the pot sink was gone. Elaine looked up from the worktable. She was pale, and she had the expression of a person watching the movements of a wild animal—attentive, focused, but unsocial, not acknowledging any returning gaze. I paused. I pressed the moment.

"Elaine, where's Max?" I said.

She should have said she didn't know and that I should wait for Mrs. Woods. Instead she said, "I think she went somewhere."

"Went somewhere?" I was beginning to sweat.

"This morning, I think she went somewhere. There was a car."

"But she didn't say anything to me," I said. "She wouldn't have gone anywhere without telling me. Unless it was going to be quick. When did she leave?"

"I don't know, ma'am."

"Did you see her leave?" I took a step toward her.

"I really don't know anything, ma'am." Then, hitting on a better approach, too late: "Mrs. Woods will be back soon, she'll know."

"I'll go find her," I said.

I turned and knocked the SERVICE door aside on my way out, so it rebounded off the wall. I shouldn't have done that. I didn't want to draw attention. I didn't want to seem like I needed to be managed just yet, and besides I was probably getting upset over nothing. Silly confusions like this must crop up every day in an estate of this size, with this many people covertly discussing each other's comings and goings. I walked down the hall with the idea that Mrs. Woods had gone to Aloysius's study, where we had seen Callisto the day before. I was practicing a furious speech for Max that I knew would be much reduced when I actually delivered it. I found the right staircase, or else an identical one, and went up. There was the door to the study, but it was closed, and nobody came when I knocked. I turned to go, then stopped and put my ear to the panel. Some suggestion of a noise.

"It's Vera," I called out.

Furniture creaked inside. I had a moment to imagine what I might be interrupting—a kaffeeklatsch of occultists, some esoteric sex act—while footsteps approached across the parquet.

Mrs. Woods opened the door. She was unhappy to see me. Behind her, at the large carved desk, was Aloysius, wearing a tennis shirt, his gleaming hair disordered. When he saw me, he leaned back and crossed his arms.

"Good morning," I said. "I'm sorry to interrupt. I'm just looking for Max."

Mrs. Woods swiveled to look at Aloysius. He said, "She left."

"What?" I said. My stomach felt cold. "Where?"

"She didn't say," Aloysius said.

"She didn't say?" I said.

He didn't repeat himself.

"You saw her leave?" I said.

He was flushed and his shirt was speckled with sweat. He smoothed his hair with one hand. His manner was immovable, uninterested, as if I were going door to door for the Jehovah's Witnesses, but I could see that he was agitated. "Yes," he said.

"In a car?"

"Yes, of course in a car."

"Her car?"

He looked confused. "What car?" he said, almost to himself, searching around on the desk. He found a glass with a little brown liquor in it, but didn't drink.

"Did she say where she was going?" I said.

"No, she didn't," he said.

"Was there—" What was the point in avoiding it? "Was there a fight this morning?"

His posture was coming undone. I thought he wouldn't answer me. But then he said, "Yes. She came in here raving. And then she drove away."

"In her car?"

"I didn't see. I thought it was a taxi." He straightened up. "I assumed she had spoken to you. I thought you would be gone by now."

I was backing out of the room. Mrs. Woods's face was fixed and her hands were tightly clasped. Aloysius looked very small in this big room; he probably thought otherwise.

I found my way, over many minutes, back to the gigantic entrance hall and out the front door onto the baking terrace. Some machinery whirred in the distance. The sun was high, the hill whitened under it. At a bend in the long driveway I saw Chuck washing a black car. I set out for the garage. Maybe she would be back soon. Maybe she had needed to clear her head, had driven to some childhood haunt. My thoughts jumped and wavered. The doors to the garage were open. Max's Avanti was still there.

I paced on the smooth concrete. I couldn't understand why she would take a taxi to wherever she was going instead of her own car. And where would she go? What place could be comforting to her here?

I had an idea, and went out to find Chuck, who had shut off the hose and was waxing the black car with a chamois cloth. I hailed him, trying to look casual.

"Did you see Max this morning?" I said.

"Max? No, I haven't seen her." He seemed normal, at ease. "Did she need a ride somewhere?"

That was another question—if she wasn't going to take her own car, why wouldn't she ask Chuck to drive her? But maybe she didn't want any of her father's staff around. "I don't know," I said. "They told me she left. But they don't know where she went."

"Huh," he said politely.

I stepped closer. "Chuck, do you know where the ranch is?"

"Oh, sure," he said. "It's about two hours up the 101 in the Santa Ynez Valley. An hour's drive from Santa Barbara, more or less. It goes on for miles."

"Do you think she could have gone there?"

"Could be."

It was a long way to go without telling me. I was chewing on my cuticles, a habit I thought I had beaten. "What about her old piano teacher?" I finally said. "Do you know where she lives?"

He looked surprised. "I, well," he said. "No, I do remember. I mean, I remember that I used to drive her to lessons." He considered, staring at the ground. "Must have been West Hollywood. Yes, she lived down there, I think."

"You don't remember where, exactly?"

"Oh, it's been so long. I remember it was a little pink house."

"Well, thank you," I said. I started to walk purposefully away from him, and then realized I didn't know where to go. I wasn't wanted here anymore, or at any rate I was more acutely unwanted than before. But I couldn't go without Max. Briefly, a certainty settled over me that she had driven off in a fit of temper and would be back soon to collect me, and we could go to a hotel and forget Il Refugio existed. What else could it possibly be? I was hungry, which made it hard to think. I climbed the

76

hill back to Delphi and searched through the cabinets until I found a box of oatmeal and a can of cling peaches. I cooked it, ate it hot out of the pan. Then I went looking for Max's purse. I couldn't find it.

By then it was noon and she had still not come. My thin hopes were growing thinner. I went out to the terrace. A white Lincoln Continental was idling in the driveway in front of the main house. While I watched, Inez hurried down the front steps, wiping her face, towing a small child by the hand. I got up and waved and yelled her name, but she didn't hear me. I set off at a jog toward the house. A man got out of the driver's side of the car and came around to get the child, who collapsed on the steps, wailing.

I was out of breath when I got to them. The man, who I gathered was Inez's husband, Roger, was negotiating tensely with the child on the steps, a blond boy whose cheeks were red from crying. A smaller girl sat placidly in the car. Inez was leaning against the fender, her face in her hands.

"Inez?" I said.

She started and gaped at me.

"Is everything all right?" I said. "I've been looking for Max."

Her face, too, was streaked with tears. She straightened up and looked uncertainly at Roger, who glanced over at us without interest. "We have to be big boys sometimes and forget about our toys," he said to the child.

"Are you leaving?" I said. "Did something happen?"

She stood there with her mouth open and then said, "I'm sorry, we have to go."

"Is it about Max?" I said.

"We have to go back to San Diego," she said.

She had some abstract sympathy for me, I thought. Because she worshipped Max and I belonged to her. I stepped closer. "Tell me what happened with Max," I said.

My presence had distracted the little boy from the problem with his toy, and Roger took advantage of his sudden quietude to scoop him up off the steps and hook the back door open.

"Is she coming back?" I said.

"We have to go," Inez said again.

Roger sailed triumphantly around the car, both children now buckled into the back seat, and got behind the wheel. "Come on," he said to Inez.

"It was nice to meet you," she said, and got into the car.

"Inez!" I said, and reached out to rap on the window. The car rolled away. I watched its slow descent down the hill, feeling the house at my back, its growing malevolence. The morning was beginning to assume the quality of a bad dream: the simple objective that could not be achieved, the shape-shifting of ordinary people.

It had been hours now. I couldn't wait here any longer. But what if she did come back and I wasn't there? I started up the hill, then stopped. What if she had gone off in a cab and gotten stuck somewhere? What if there had been an accident? What if she had gone to the ocean and drowned? What could keep her for all these hours? The thought of waiting in the guesthouse while something terrible happened to her was unbearable. I went back to Delphi and hunted around the room we had shared, and there it was: her handbag. Our Pan Am tickets back home were inside, and her keys. She had left everything. No—her money clip, where she carried her cash and driver's license, wasn't there. She often put the money clip in her pocket rather than her purse. I searched through the clothes on the floor for it but couldn't find it. I hoped she had taken it with her.

I shoved my things in my suitcase, changed into the more practical of the two pairs of shoes I had brought, and left a note on the bed, just in case, that said *I left to look for you, call my service.* She knew the number. I found a telephone in the hall and called the service myself to leave a message for her: "I'm going to the ranch to look for you. I'll check messages tonight if I possibly can." The girl read the message back to me. "Yes, thank you," I said, and hung up the phone.

Back outside, struggling with Max's suitcase and my own, I found Chuck still working on the black car, going at the chrome with a chamois cloth and a tin of polish. I shuffled through scenarios, thinking which would be the least interesting to him.

"She just called from a restaurant downtown," I said, affecting embarrassment at my earlier confusion. "I'm going to go meet her for lunch. She said to take the Avanti."

Chuck straightened up. "You don't want me to drive you?"

"Oh no, and wait around all afternoon? We might go to the beach."

"All right, if you're sure."

"Is there gas in it?" I said.

"Oh, I keep them all ready to go."

"Terrific," I said.

I entered the garage and went along the line to the silver-blue car in the back. It vibrated faintly with Max's presence. I put the bags in the trunk, got in, and felt the pedals. The car smelled like mink oil. The keys were where Max had left them, behind the sun visor. I wondered if Aloysius would report the car stolen. It wasn't my car, but it wasn't his either. Was the California Highway Patrol likely to care about my explanations—the friend from New York? If Chuck had not been out there in the driveway, I would have just driven it away and hoped that it took some time for a household like this to notice something as trivial as a missing car. But that was not how things had gone. I put the key in the ignition and the engine turned over. It had a wonderful sound, a deep, assured thrum. I had some disloyal thoughts about my beleaguered old Chevy, waiting for me back in Brooklyn.

The Avanti had more power than I was used to, and as I shifted into first it surged forward, almost clipping the bumper of the coupe in the next row. I guided the car down the side aisle of the barn and out into the glaring sunlight, waving at Chuck, with more of a grin than I'd intended. I was moving. I was getting away.

CHAPTER 7

I drove out of Bel Air, out of the zone of hedges and gatehouses. I felt my heart rate slow as the road sloped downhill and then flattened and widened, and the world assumed its normal character again, with commerce indifferently displayed and people indifferently housed. I passed dry cleaners and Mexican groceries and car washes and the occasional Woolworth's. In the spaces between, networks of tract houses bloomed like algae over the dry flats. At a stoplight, a man in the next car stared admiringly at the Avanti, and I wished there had been something less noticeable to drive.

In time the tract houses dwindled and the road passed through a series of small towns, bright stucco and wood-frame houses that clung together at the foot of bare hills. When I had been driving for an hour, the highway touched down at the edge of the ocean, and I drove along the beach, the windows down, the wind battering through the car. Max must have come this way so many times in back seats, as a child with her family. She would have driven through the same surfing villages, passed the same beaches. I was reassured by the Pacific and wasn't sure why. It wasn't familiar and it didn't remind me of home. But it made the landscape so legible. You can't be disoriented beside an ocean.

Once I had put some distance between myself and Il Refugio, I felt safe enough to stop and study the map. I pulled off the road and parked in a patch of sandy gravel, fronted by a game little guardrail that faced the Pacific. At the other end of this makeshift lot, a woman sat with her driver's side door open and both feet on the ground, knocking sand out of her shoe. There was no one else around but the bright dots of a few surfers against a headland farther north. The air felt good. My sense of doom had lifted slightly. This would all be straightened out soon. She would be at the ranch, or if she wasn't, I could find a telephone there and call my service, and she would have left me a message by then. Maybe she was waiting at a hotel in some more manageable neighborhood already. She would still be imperious, from everything that had happened, and I would soothe her for an afternoon and she would wake up the next morning back to her normal self, making jokes about it. Or maybe she would be frank about her sadness. Maybe it was time for that. We could both be better at that. When she had mentioned my mother, that had stung—of course it had, of course she'd known it would. She must have just wanted me to tell her these things, share these old hurts, like I wanted her to. We were idiots, the pair of us. Long defended against obsolete enemies—the parents whose roofs we no longer lived under, the teenage peers for whom we had exhausted ourselves pantomiming heterosexuality. We had gotten in the habit of mystery, and now we didn't know how to drop it. We played a hand of easily guessed cards very close to our vests.

Peach had gone to a workshop for a weekend in Cold Spring the summer before and had come back talking about honoring her truth and Sylvia's truth, and Sylvia told me later that now, once a week, they lit a candle on their coffee table and set out a bowl of fruit, whose meaning was symbolic in some way I couldn't remember, and faced each other and held hands and repeated phrases about acceptance, and that these episodes were supposed to culminate in an honest, nonjudgmental, loving expression of whatever grievance happened to be on either of their minds that week, and that Sylvia thought it was batty but it was important to Peach so she had started inventing grievances to share, the same way she had made up minor sins to confess to the priest when she was a child. It worked best if she told Peach she was upset because Peach had not been adequately present in some way. Peach was a small hurricane of affection and anxious contact and loved nothing more than to be told that more affection and contact were needed.

Nick, my friend from the Dominican Republic job, had been in analysis for years. He talked easily about his relationships and how he felt, using an argot that I barely understood about his complexes and those of others and the ways that one thing stood for another in other people's lives. But there was still some restraint there. I had noticed that people who swore by analysis were more closemouthed in general than the people I knew who had gone to workshops or spent weekends in ashrams or sweat lodges in the Catskills or taken Transcendental

Meditation classes from one of the many robed figures who now appeared downtown, in Union Square and Washington Square Park. Those people were more likely to clasp my hands, to ask how I was *really* doing. At a dinner party that I had gone to with Max a month or two back, there had been a tarot card reader. I liked tarot cards, actually; they were beautiful, and the reader was beautiful too, a tall woman with a lot of gray in her hair, carefully dressed, glinting with silver jewelry. I had stood off to one side, and Max had taken my shyness for skepticism.

"You're an absolute nun," she had said fondly.

"Nuns are mystics," I said. "I love having my fortune told."

I waited to the end, after everyone else had drifted back to the hi-fi and the kitchen, and then the reader pulled a few cards for me. I couldn't remember now what they said. It didn't make much of an impression at the time, something about looking forward and not back. There was the one with a man holding a bundle of sticks. Earlier, someone had pulled the death card and *oooh*s ran around the room. "It's only change," the reader had said, "it's only change."

I got out and unfolded the map across the hood, where the breeze off the ocean rattled its edges. Short, tough flowers grew along the guardrail. It was a simple drive, like Chuck had said, taking the 101 up to the San Marcos Pass Road, which was Route 154, and into the Santa Ynez Valley. I had no idea where in the valley to go. I would have to stop and ask for directions to the ranch when I got close. But I was hopeful. There weren't many roads in the valley to choose from. I squinted close at one—Refugio Road. Refugio, Ynez. The Comstocks could be sentimental. I folded up the map and leaned against the car. The air was sticky, and the humidity was welcome after a day up in the hills. Surf broke around an outcropping of black rock a hundred yards offshore. I stood and thought about the Atlantic, its hostile little waves at Rockaway, its featureless broad beaches, the sideways drag of its current across the revelers at Coney Island. After a few minutes I realized I was being observed: a pair of sea lions bobbed out past the breakers, patiently watching me.

I got back in and started up the car again. On impulse, I rifled through the glove box until I found the registration and unfolded it. There was the name: Evangeline Coretta Comstock.

I read it several times, baffled. The breeze made it struggle in my hands; I rolled up the windows. Her mother, I thought finally. This must be Max's mother's name. They changed the registration after Max left.

I leaned back and closed my eyes. I will do my very best, I thought. I will have to do my very best not to get stopped by the police.

There was nothing else to do. It was done now, I had already taken it, and I wasn't going back. I pulled back onto the road and worked my way up through the gears. The highway rose and dipped, sometimes tracing the edge of the bluffs above the water, sometimes coming back down to run along the beaches.

I distracted myself from worry about the accidental theft of the car with thoughts of my work back home. Business had been good lately. Word got around. My friends, my circle, were not the type who generally had much luck in front of judges, but if they came in with a sheaf of papers and photos they'd gotten from me, sometimes it went better. Alternatively, I could give them information to convince the other party that going to court wasn't worth it in the first place. I'd recently helped a friend of a friend with a custody case—her ex-husband wanted to keep her from seeing the kids, and was prepared to tell the family court judge about her girlfriend. As it turned out, he was running an insurance scam out of three states, which was not all that difficult to uncover, and when he was presented with evidence of his activities, he decided that he was satisfied with visitation after all. I had enjoyed that case, even though there had been some threats at the end, and I had to watch my rearview mirror for a few weeks after it was over. It was nice to feel like I was helping somebody, once in a while.

Max knew everybody and could be a terrific source of information, although I tried to keep her out of my work. The owner of the Bracken had to deal with the mob, like everybody else running gay bars downtown, so there were faces that Max knew, groups of men who swept in sometimes just before the place opened at four o'clock or just before it closed at two, who disappeared into the office upstairs and left out the back. She could read the weather of the Village from these visits. If the men left looking irritated, a raid would follow soon after. The mob passed the bars off to the cops for punishment when their protection payments were late. The police would run a perfunctory raid and collect their own take, and then pass them back to the mob. So Max, behind the bar, stood at the nexus of all this, and saw everything. She could take care of herself. I rarely saw her shaken. She threw drunks out on her own, blackballed hustlers who stole tips, and broke up the occasional fight by waving the bat they kept on the bottom shelf behind the bar. And yet I worried about her all the time.

In Santa Barbara I took the turnoff for 154, and the highway turned away from the coast and up into the low mountains. It was noisy with the windows down, but too hot with them up. Route 154 was smaller than 101, and I passed painted signs indicating that there were farms hidden in the foothills, among the scrub. An irrigation system spread across the flats near a riverbed where only a narrow channel of water ran. There was so much empty space. I wasn't used to it. The landscape had an exposed look. The mountains were bare. I looked out for the San Marcos Pass, expecting the road to squeeze through a chink in the rock and reveal a long view of a valley, an image I had probably gotten from some spaghetti Western, but no such thing happened. I noticed only that the blacktop was descending again and concluded that this was the Santa Ynez Valley. I saw few other cars. Pastures spread out on both sides of the road, and far off I occasionally saw cattle, but little else. The mountains subsided into an undulating blue line in the distance. I was grateful to Chuck for the full tank. It seemed like the kind of place where you could run out of gas and be stuck for a while. The sun poured in the side window, and I wondered if my arm would burn.

I pulled over and looked at the map again. There was a town called Santa Ynez, just off the main road a few miles on. I kept going until I saw the turnoff, and then bumped along for a few minutes, past scattered ranch houses, until I saw a gas station sharing a parking lot with a luncheonette. I was hungry. I pulled in, topped off the gas tank just to be safe, and parked in front of the restaurant, a tiny flat-roofed box with an oversized sign: HOME COOKING.

There were a few other patrons in the restaurant. The sound of a sprayer in the kitchen dominated. A pair of old men chatted in a booth, and a woman who smelled like she had just come from getting a permanent rinse sat alone at the short counter, staring over the rim of a coffee cup at nothing in particular. I sat at the other end and ordered hash browns, which I could see in a golden pile on the flattop grill, and a couple of sausages, which I thought would be cooked fast. I was worried about police. I didn't like the idea of sitting there too long with a flashy car in the lot, not in a small town like this. For all I knew, the Comstocks had a direct line to the cops in this county. The more I reflected on it, the more I thought it would be surprising if they didn't. So it came down to whether they had spoken to Chuck yet, whether they had noticed the car was gone. And now, of course, I had to ask an indiscreet question.

"Hey," I said when the man behind the counter brought my coffee. "You know how to get to the Comstock place?"

"The ranch?" he said. "You get back out on the 154, keep heading north, and take the next right turn after the creek in two or three miles. Then it's pretty much all Comstock land."

I thanked him and repeated the directions to myself a few times. When the food came, I ate quickly and left a big tip, although not so big as to call attention.

I found the road the man had described without much difficulty. Roads were few and far between out here. It was after three o'clock by then, and the light was changing. It was a relief to be off the highway, which traversed the valley floor in a straight line and was visible for miles around. Trees crowded closer together along this little road, and the slopes of the San Rafael foothills pressed in. The clarity of the afternoon had a silvery cast. The shadows of the trees were deep.

In the end, I took a chance on a driveway. I bumped along on gravel for ten minutes, fifteen, beginning to regret it as nothing appeared. I drove through wild fields of yellow grass, dotted with oaks. A split-rail fence ran along beside me. At last the driveway ended in a dirt roundabout, and I stopped. Below me was the Santa Ynez River, winding through rocky shallows, and to my left, through trees, I could see a white house.

I parked the car and sat, preparing myself. It was very quiet without the sound of the engine. A breeze moved in the grass. I could hear the river. The heat of the day was fragile. It would be cold when the sun set. My lips felt dry, my face windburned from driving with the windows down. I gathered my things, spent a minute staring at Max's purse, and then hid it in the back seat.

The house was large and low, a ranch house in the original sense, spreading across a flat patch of land just above the river, with a porch across its wide front. I saw no one as I approached, moving through the shadows of eucalyptus trees, thinking about Max and her brother and sister here as children. Had they stayed in this house? Were there other houses on the thousands of acres? An ancient rope swing swayed in a light breeze. I stepped onto the porch, which creaked, and faced the front door. A wind chime sounded somewhere to my right. I rang the bell and then knocked as well, a habit from Brooklyn, where you were never sure if anybody's buzzer worked. Nobody came. The house did not disarrange itself in any way. I tried again, and

89

walked down to the end of the porch while I waited, glancing at the windows as I passed. There was no movement, no noise.

Then I heard voices. I went down the porch steps and around the side of the house, which was larger than I would have guessed from the front. Some flower beds had gone to seed and spread into the yard. To my right, the land sloped down to the riverbank, and I flinched at a flash of white from that direction: an egret, which flew away with languid wing-beats. I was tense. If I encountered anyone but Max, I would have to bluster and improvise.

I came out into the clearing behind the house. It took me a moment to understand what I was looking at. A field of dry grass extended to a distant slope. A small group of people stood in a semicircle with their backs to the house, and a hundred yards beyond them was a black figure in the field with two goats on leads. The figure, I saw as she shifted to scratch her neck, was a woman in a black cape with a loose hood, like a sinister monk in an Italian novel. The group close to the house was equipped with a camera on a tripod, some boxes and crates, and a lighting umbrella. They were shooting a movie. I stopped there and watched.

"One more time!" yelled the man with the camera, and the figure deflated and then gathered herself, pulling the hood back into position. She trotted toward the cameras, pulling the goats behind her, and then turned toward the hill again and waited. "Action!" he shouted, and she walked slowly away from them, ceremoniously, pausing on each step. The goat on the right was distracted by forage. The woman tugged on the rope without turning her head. Someone in the semicircle giggled but stifled it.

They were mostly men, but a few women straggled at the outside of the group, two of them smoking together. One turned and saw me, without surprise. She took me in for a second and then opened her hand: a waggling little wave, raised eyebrows, amused. She turned back to her friend before I could respond. She had a shocking face. They both did. Actresses, I thought. They were dressed in white and the sun was coming through it.

A man from the other end of the line turned and headed for the house, hands in pockets. He squinted at me. When he was close, he said, "Hello. Kate's friend?"

"Oh," I said. "No." I was aware of what I was wearing: a summer dress that was almost ten years old, which I had chosen for this trip because it had the distinction of reaching my knees. It had a Peter Pan collar and it made me look like a kindergarten teacher, or a repressed personal secretary. He was dressed in a version of what I had come to think of as the painter's uniform: a very faded button-front, half-undone, with the kind of impervious canvas pants you could wrestle a steer in. There were a lot of men wandering around the Village like this, coming and going from the New School, dressed for farm labor, with paint on their cracked boots. I felt all of my thirty years. It was hard to guess whether my getup would make me seem guileless or simply foreign and strange. "I'm looking for Max," I said, and then, impulsively, "I'm Max's girlfriend. Is she here?"

He was unfazed, or pretended to be. "Max? She's one of the girls?"

"Max Comstock. One of the Comstocks."

"Oh. I don't think I've met any Comstocks."

There it was again, real fear, prickling along the bottom of my brain. I made a noise, some kind of gasping little sigh. He was staring at me. "I don't know where she is," I said.

He took a step backward and glanced at the house, uncomfortable. "Well, it's a big place, though. Maybe one of the cabins or something?"

"Cabins?"

"There are cabins all down the valley for the cattle hands."

"Okay," I said, "thanks." Why would she drive all the way out here and stay in a cabin? But no—a little hope. Maybe she did it because the house was occupied. Maybe she wanted to be alone. She didn't know these people.

The shoot was beginning to break up. The woman in the cloak was making the long walk back toward the group, leaving the goats behind in the field. The director, a short and solid man with a wave of gray hair, was talking to his crew. The smell of marijuana drifted across the grass.

"Can I use the telephone?" I said.

The inside of the house was a combination of austerity and largeness of scale that I recognized as the rustic end of the *Town & Country* idea. The man led me down an improbably long front hallway, paneled in old boards, past an immense kitchen where a battalion of pans hung on the wall behind a range and a woodstove, past two or three rooms filled with chairs, to a telephone on a hall table. I thanked him and he wandered off. I dialed my service, worrying about the high charge for a transcontinental call, then hoping that such calls were being made often enough that it would not be noticed on the bill. The crowd outside all looked like long-distance callers.

A girl picked up and I said, "Hello, this is Vera Kelly, account 402. Any messages?"

The pause was long enough for me to imagine all kinds of resolutions to this nightmare. But she came back on the line and said, "No new messages, ma'am."

"Are you sure?"

"Account 402? Nothing new."

I hung up and stood there, hands at my sides, looking down the hallway at a window at the end, through which I could see a slice of yellow hill. She had not come back and she had not called. She would have known to call the service. She left messages for me there all the time—letting me know she would be working late, telling me about food she had left for me in the refrigerator.

I could call the police. But I knew they wouldn't do anything. They would think it was a lovers' spat. The thought of having to explain my fear to a leering cop made my skin crawl.

I turned and headed back toward the front of the house. At a corner I was stopped short by the director, who stepped into my path and then lurched back.

"Oh, I'm sorry," I said.

"No problem," he muttered. His eyes were red. He looked about fifty, and I grasped that he was profoundly stoned. From one of the large sitting rooms, I heard talk and laughter.

"You haven't seen Maxine Comstock, have you?" I said, holding out hope that the first man I'd spoken to wasn't up to date.

The director was shorter than I was. I recognized the suspicion with which older men processed this fact. He was processing it slowly. "Maxine?" he said.

"Maxine Comstock," I said. "Aloysius's daughter."

He looked alarmed. "Aloysius's daughter! Is she here?"

"That's what I'm asking you," I said. "I'm looking for her."

"Oh," he said. He glanced toward the sitting room. "I haven't seen her." Then he came up with something and pulled himself together around it. "If you see her!" he said. "Please tell her! That we would love to involve her in our project."

"Your movie?" I said.

"We would love to," he said again, leaning close for emphasis, and then he walked away.

I didn't have the nerve yet to face a whole room full of these strangers, so I set off around the periphery of the house, looking for a lone person I could ask for directions down to the cabins. I saw a shadow through the front door and stepped out. It was one of the actresses, smoking a cigarette and leaning against the porch post. Her ankles were crossed. She looked like Faye Dunaway with flat-ironed hair. She revolved to look at me.

"H-hello," I said. I wasn't handling California very well; I wasn't casual enough about these armies of beautiful women. Max was so beautiful that all of us girls at the bar who adored her, in the days before she inexplicably picked me, had felt mocked and baited by her presence. But this was the world she was from, and her unselfconsciousness was genuine. I wanted to apologize to the woman in front of me for interrupting her doing nothing. "I'm looking for Maxine Comstock. Has she been here?" I said.

She smiled. "Nobody here but us chickens."

"Somebody said there were some cabins," I said. "I thought she might be there."

"Oh, that's right," she said. "George and Carlos spent the night out there, a few nights ago, so they could trip by themselves."

"Do you know how to get there?"

She ashed her cigarette over the porch rail. "It's cross-country on a horse. Do you ride?"

Despair. What a question. "No, I don't ride."

"Oh," she said. "Well, I don't think you can drive there. I'm sorry."

I had to go out to the car to think what to do next. The air was growing cool. The river insisted more loudly in the warm air. I admitted to myself how thin the limb I stood on was. She had been gone for hours and hours now. It would be cruel to do that and not call, and she wasn't cruel. I started to panic again, struggling to get mouthfuls of air. When we first got together, I had become preoccupied with gas leaks and radon and falling air conditioners. My good fortune was impossible and I expected it to be taken away. A small, evil voice in the back of my head now said, *You see?*

I decided to go back in and call hospitals. Something to do. And then I would see if somebody could take me to the cabins tomorrow. I could sleep in the car tonight. I could sleep on the ground. I hardly had a body right then. It didn't matter.

Back in the house, I found a couple of fat directories in the drawer under the telephone, one for Los Angeles County and one for Santa Barbara County. I sat on the floor and called all the hospitals one by one. People passed by me and glanced down, but no one spoke to me. I waited on the line while young women checked the census. Again and again they said, "No, ma'am, no one here by that name."

I reached the end of the list and leaned back against the wall, trying to decide if I was relieved. Faye Dunaway appeared again.

"Hey there," she said, crouching, her golden arms crossed. "You should come get something to eat."

"Oh," I said. Speech was not working well for me. I was like a man discovered on a desert island. "Oh." Then, after a rigid pause: "Thank you."

She extended a hand to help me up. "Listen, you're really worried about her?"

"Yes," I said. "We're—" She was looking at me kindly and I wanted to offer an explanation. "We live in New York. We came out to LA to see her family. But now she's gone."

"She'll turn up," the actress said. "People just lose their minds out here."

Dishes were laid out on a trestle table in one of the big rooms, and the crowd milled around. There were fifteen or twenty people there, filling stoneware plates, choosing seats on the floor or in artfully battered old chairs. One of the actresses had forgone a plate and lay on a side table instead, one knee up, blowing smoke rings at the ceiling. There were a lot of garbanzo beans, and a large bowl of noodles, and something with eggplant and tomato sauce that was not quite a parmigiana. Once my plate was filled, I wanted to vanish into the hallway or kitchen, but I needed to mix and ingratiate myself and ask questions. My mind stuck again on the unfashionable dress I was wearing. The men were in army surplus and Italian boots. One of the women was in Pucci. And there was my hair, which looked frayed in the dry air, the curls forgetting what they were about. I had pinned it all back punitively in the car. I decided not to smile too much. At one end of the room was a huge fireplace. I sat on a stump that had been placed ostentatiously beside it with a hatchet for splitting kindling. A projector had been set up, aimed at the plaster wall opposite.

Who were these people? The question seemed too large and diffuse to approach. Who had given them permission to be here? Aloysius, I had to assume. Maybe they were more of the "awful people" that Inez had been complaining about, like the ones who had been occupying the bigger guesthouse right before we arrived. A young man was sitting near me, a downy-looking kid, and I leaned over and said, "How do you all know the family?"

"The family?" His eyes turned anxiously toward me.

"The Comstocks," I said.

"Oh," he said. "I think they're financing the film."

"Oh."

"They're friends with the guy who wrote the movie." He looked panicked. I wondered if he was high.

"Ah," I said. "St. James."

"Is that his name?"

"I have a feeling it is," I said. "What's the movie about?"

"What?"

"The movie. What's it about?"

"Consciousness."

"Oh. It—?" I tried for a follow-up question but came up empty.

"And sex. Sex and consciousness." He was picking up speed. "And there's a lot of things with animals. Mostly the animals that are here because that's what we can get. Goats and horses and cows. But they represent all animals."

"All animals," I said.

"All animals," he said. He returned to his plate.

The director came in, even more red-eyed than before, and stood with his feet planted in front of the food table. He was stocky, round-bellied, with a sunburned patch of chest showing. "Beautiful work today," he said, applauding. Some people set down their plates and applauded back. "Beautiful, beautiful. Marie—Tom—" He gestured to the woman on the table and a man sitting in a chair nearby. "This afternoon in the river. That was something. I won't forget that."

Tom nodded graciously, eyes closed.

"They don't like to see us get this kind of work down on film," he said. "They're not going to be happy. But more and more people are waking up. I'm not as young as most of you. They weren't making films in Kenosha, Wisconsin, in 1935," he went on. "When I got my first camera. Little Brownie camera. I'll tell you that. Nobody was making art in Kenosha, Wisconsin. The distance from here to there—when I tell you I grew up on Mars. I grew up on Mars! Many of you did too." I had the feeling that this speech was familiar, and that the rest of his audience was better equipped than I was to put the fragments of it together when pieces were missing, as they seemed to be now. "It's a long bus ride, isn't it? A very long bus ride to the old Pacific Greyhound terminal. And now we're in the stars."

Activity was resuming. The director roused himself to indicate that he was not finished.

"We need to address something," he said. "Negativity." He looked around. "Black, black hearts. Usually on the outside. But sometimes—today was one of those times—sometimes you see it here. Negativity. Bad wavelength. You point it out, you make it grow. You don't point it out, maybe it grows faster. Very bad molecular behavior. We all saw it."

"It's okay, Cliff, he left," somebody said.

"He went back to Santa Monica," said Marie from the table.

"Good riddance," said the director. "But it's important for us to remember that it could be any one of us. Any one of us could give in."

He relinquished his spot, put his hand on the trestle table as if thinking about having something to eat, but wandered back out into the hallway instead. Eating and talking resumed.

"Something happened today?" I said to the kid next to me.

"Just a fight," he said, working his jaw. "There's been a fight every three days for the last two weeks."

I decided to make an attempt. How else could I start? Stand up and give an announcement?

"Hey," I said. "I'm looking for somebody to help me get out to the cabins tomorrow."

He shrank away. "I'm a grip," he said. "I'm working."

"Sure, of course," I said, collapsing.

"You have to ride a horse," he said.

"That's what I've heard."

The man I had spoken to first was threading film into the projector. Someone switched off the lights. The machine threw a white square of light on the wall, touching the edge of a window frame. There was a title card and a long panning shot across eucalyptus trees backlit by the sun. Everyone was watching with rapt attention.

"Is this—" I whispered.

"It's what we got last month," said the young man, impatiently.

The mixing and sound had not been done yet, and the landscape shots were silent, with occasional breathing and rustling. It made me apprehensive, as if I were standing next to a person who wouldn't speak to me. The shots were long. The cuts were ragged. At one point the camera rushed, rattling, down a long hill—it must have been on wheels—and everyone cheered. We watched a dead lizard for a while. Then Marie and Tom were standing on a footbridge over a creek. Marie said, "Nobody ever hears it twice." Tom slapped her. A moment later they were having sex in the creek—a confusing series of close-ups—and Tom was pushing her face underwater.

It was at this point that I decided I would be better off somewhere else, where I could be miserable and afraid without watching straight people have dyspeptic sex. I got up as quietly as I could and made my way around the back of the room. Marie struggled on the screen. The live Marie had come down from the table and was sitting on the floor with her arms around her knees. "Here it's going to be cut with the butterfly scene," someone said. "Hey, go easy on her, Tom," somebody else said, and everyone laughed. I set my empty plate on the edge of the trestle table. The director stood in the doorway, watching the film with his arms crossed. I stepped past him into the dark hallway, and he started and pivoted.

"You," he said.

I stopped. I wanted to go and call my service again.

"Does Aloysius know you're here?" he said.

I hesitated. The director could easily call and find out.

"Did the wife send you?" he said.

"The wife?" I was backing away.

"Did the county send you?" he said.

"No," I said. "I'm looking for Maxine. I told you."

We stood staring at each other in the flickering light of the movie. A semi-orgasmic scream drawled out into the hall.

"I have to make a phone call," I said. "Excuse me."

"St. James knows about all of you," the director said. "So don't worry about that."

"Okay!" I said. I pushed past him. My heart had accelerated again. His paranoia followed me down the hall. I didn't want to turn, but I was sure he was watching me. I wondered if there was cocaine around the place. He had that sweaty, furious air. I dialed the familiar numbers. A night-shift girl came on.

"Vera Kelly, account 402," I said.

"Thank you, please hold," she said.

I looked up the hall, holding the receiver to my face. The director was gone. I rubbed my eyebrows with my thumb and forefinger. I was so tired.

"One new message," she said. "Logged at 6:55 PM, New York time. The caller is Max Comstock. Shall I read it?"

"Oh, thank God," I said. Tears sprang into my eyes. For a few seconds I couldn't recall how to direct my breathing and speak at the same time.

"Miss Kelly? Shall I read it?"

"Please do," I said, gasping.

"It reads, 'I'm in Mineral Springs Hospital. Mineral Springs Hospital.' There's a note—it says she spelled it out and then she was disconnected."

"That's all?"

"That's all it says."

If there had been an accident—what was Mineral Springs, I had called every hospital in the book—could it be in another county, not Los Angeles or Santa Barbara but Ventura or even Orange—had I been wrong to guess she had driven north? But she was alive and talking. I was crying in earnest now. The night shift girl waited on the line. "Where is that?" I said. "Where is it?"

"Miss?"

"The hospital," I said, knowing there was no reason the night-shift girl at the message service in Midtown Manhattan should know. "Where is Mineral Springs Hospital?"

"Should I connect you to information, miss?"

"No, no," I said. "I don't have a city to give them."

"All right. Anything else?"

"No. Thank you," I said, fervently, but she had already clicked off.

I floated toward the kitchen. I was flushed, my hands shaking with relief. A couple of handsome young men were in there, leaning against the counters, flanking Faye Dunaway at the stove. Another sat at a table. She said, "But isn't it such a *bore*?"

"Thanks for dinner," I said from the doorway, and then, because she'd been kind earlier, "She just left me a message."

"Oh, wonderful!" she said. "Going to bed?"

The two young men looked over at me uneasily. It was the look that men give a rival, not an object of interest. It was funny that this happened sometimes, that young straight men could read me when I thought I was incognito among them. I had grown into it, maybe. I was more transparent at thirty than I had been at twenty. It made them unfriendly.

"Heading out," I said. I didn't know where, but I also knew I couldn't stay now that I had heard her voice. Something would come to me. A next step.

I felt a presence and turned to see the director.

"You stole that car," he said.

Faye and the two men looked up, with some interest. I blinked. "I don't—"

"I just called," the director said. "They put me right through to Aloysius. You stole that car."

Would technicalities serve me? Probably not. "It's Max's car. It was given to her."

"Who's Max?" said one of the young men at the table.

"Negativity," said the director. "It's the wife, isn't it?"

"I've never met the wife," I said. I was still in the doorway, but I stepped backward into the hall. I was fairly sure there was an unobstructed path behind me to the front door, although I didn't turn to look. Amplified rustling sounds came from the room where the movie was playing.

"There are always saboteurs," said the director.

Faye and the two men were watching this neutrally. I wondered how many other expulsions they had witnessed during this shoot. "It's not stolen," I said. "Good night." I turned and walked away. My face was burning. The only question was whether he had called the police. I hoped he hadn't had time. He must have been on another line while I was using the telephone down the hall. A house this deep in the country with two lines! I turned right and went out the front door. The night air was cool and smelled like grass. The sky was deep black, and I could see the Milky Way, a glittering smear over the hill

103

across the river. I walked with quick steps across the packed dirt and gravel to the little car. There was a trill in my ears. Would they follow me? How far was the director willing to go to ingratiate himself with Aloysius? Pretty far, I guessed. I fumbled the keys in the door and dropped into the front seat. A frantic drive in '68, in an unfamiliar car in the Dominican countryside, came back to me all at once. The unpleasant, bitter taste of adrenaline. The engine turned over and I found the headlights, very grateful now for my foresight in topping off the gas tank. In the rearview mirror, I saw the front door of the house open and the porch light come on. I took the car in a wide turn and bumped back out onto the dirt track.

I didn't have much of an idea except to get back out onto the main highway and find a motel for the night. It could be miles and miles. And I didn't want to drive back down toward Santa Barbara—if somebody was looking for me, they'd be coming from that way. I would go north up the 101. I shook the road atlas out of the glove compartment and held it on my knees, too nervous to stop or look down for a good half hour. Then I pulled over to the shoulder, surrounded by the black shadows of a stand of trees, and consulted the book.

After two hours I stopped at a motel, a sign glowing blue-white in front of a minimal one-story arrangement in white stucco. I pulled in and saw, to my relief, that the parking lot extended around one side of the low building, so that a few spaces between the motel itself and the small outbuilding marked OFFICE were shielded from the view of passing eyes. I parked the car in this small harbor and checked my compact mirror. I looked like I had been packed in a suitcase. I was wrinkled and flattened, and my eyes had the haunted and disreputable look of a person who has been driving alone too long. I arranged my hair with my fingers and practiced a few normal expressions.

I was in the mountains again, at the straggling end of a small town. The rocky peaks bore down on me in the dark. There were so many mountain ranges in California, saints' names piled on saints' names. Too much geography. A couple of rooms were lit, the curtains drawn. The voice of a television ventured out into the huge quiet. I hurried into the office, where a teenage night clerk took my money and handed me the keys to room 107.

The door gave without any trouble. The room was done in pink and beige. The door to the bathroom hung sideways, one hinge broken. There was a television. The place smelled like disinfectant, which I decided, after a minute, was reassuring. I sat on the bed and pulled off my shoes.

She must have driven hours in a temper and then gotten into an accident. What else could it be?

But then why would the call be so short and so cryptic?

Maybe she was concussed. Medicated. Coming out of surgery. Alone—I started to cry. I was so tired.

There was a pay phone in the parking lot. I went back out with a handful of change and called my service again. No new messages.

Back in the room, I lay on the nylon bedspread and stared at the ceiling. I left the bedside lamp on, and most of my clothes. I hadn't reconciled myself to getting under the sheets. It was too intimate, and the Clorox caught in my nose. The bulb in the lamp was weak and the room was mostly in shadow. I didn't turn on my television, but I could hear the murmur of the one next door through the wall, and from time to time there were slow, heavy footsteps treading back and forth from the bathroom to the bed.

In the morning I would call Nick, my reporter friend. He would have some ideas. How do you find a hospital when you don't know the city, the county? I could call information and just list off all the cities I could think of in driving distance from Los Angeles—even though she could have driven for hours, and there were hundreds of towns and cities she could have passed through. No matter, I could start there, I had nothing but time. I could get an operator on the line and test her patience. Read through the names in the road atlas one by one until she cut me off.

I would call Nick. I would have to tell him what had happened, and he would worry. Thinking of his worry seized me with fear again. That she was mangled forever, that she would die. That I would never find her.

And she had run off, hadn't she? She had left me there this morning.

This thought was unbearable and made me furious with myself. In a panic I sat up on the bed and pulled Max's suitcase over from where I had left it on a chair. My eyes were very dry and hot. I dug through her things. Inside the shirt box there was her sheaf of staff paper, and separately, clipped together in a folder, the libretto for her opera. I held it to my face. She had driven away and left me. She had tired of me. She had seen that I was no use to her in the place she came from. We had left our home, and in the absence of our routines, the thread that connected us had grown so fine that it snapped.

These were stupid things to think, and I tried to get myself under control. She hadn't wanted me to read her work, and I thought at first that maybe I would be satisfied just with holding it, knowing the hours she had spent with it. But I wasn't. I opened the folder.

ANGELUS

OR, SISTER AIMEE IN THE DESERT

There was a photo cut from a magazine of Aimee Semple McPherson in a beaded white gown, posed ecstatically in a stage doorway against a celestial light.

I rolled over in the bed, my back turned defensively to the door as if Max herself might catch me reading it. I knew McPherson had been a preacher and drove people wild in Los Angeles in the twenties. And Max had told me the story about her coming to the Comstock patriarch to ask for money to build the Angelus Temple. That was about all I knew. The text marched down the middle of the page in squares of blank verse. Aimee sat in a bar in Agua Prieta, Mexico, *wreathed in smoke*. She addressed the audience. She was born in a village in Ontario, she told them. She felt the calling early. Her mother guided her in Christ. She married young and was widowed at twenty. She married again, a mistake. She went out on the road; she spoke in tongues and healed people. She came to Los Angeles, alone with her children. The phrasing was simple, with a steady meter that surfaced here and there. I flipped to the staff paper, wanting to know what the music would be doing underneath the words, but of course I could make no sense of it. I thought of Max being angry with me for going through her things, and more than anything the thought comforted me. I could confess this transgression when I found her.

Aimee preached to growing crowds. She built the Angelus Temple, by *gifts of faith / and an oilman*. I smiled to see Max put her grandfather into it, in this tiny way. Tourists poured into the Angelus Temple, and Aimee put a radio station inside to broadcast the services, with *two antenna towers on the roof / where a belfry might have been*. The sanctuary was made in the form of a theater, with balconies and a sloped floor. Max's stage directions described a set within the set, with Aimee standing in the wings of her own production as the panels slid back and forth under a glittering curtain. The light should be *very bright, very yellow*. A note in the margin in Max's neat diagonal hand read, *Recordings extant?*

Aimee was famous, rich, and powerful. Her nerves frayed. She had her own desires. She had divorced her second husband, but she encouraged an impression that she was a pious widow instead of a divorcée. She was a widow after all, she said defensively: *I buried a husband.* She began an affair with a recording engineer in her radio station, a married man. She was sick with love, not sleeping. If anyone found out, her ministry would collapse. She had two young children. Aimee, sitting again in the Mexican bar at the left of the stage, sang,

> *I had to get away*
> *Get away*
> *I could think of nothing else*

The stage directions said, *Soft sounds of surf.*

Then Aimee:

I went swimming

The ocean grew louder. The congregants from the earlier preaching scenes returned to the stage and stood looking out at the audience, crowded together, *searching the waves.* The lights came down. Max had written in the margin, *Lights go slowly.*

The room was cold. I wrapped the comforter around myself. I didn't get up to undress or brush my teeth. I turned off the lamp and lay in the dark for a while, listening to the television through the wall.

CHAPTER 8

I was awake early. The room was frigid. I brushed my teeth and took a dribbling shower as hot as I could get it. Once every twenty minutes or so, a tractor trailer passed by outside, downshifting on the grade of the highway where it turned and rose in front of the motel. Apart from that, there was nothing to break the hush but the vascular hissing and popping of the motel plumbing. I dumped my purse out on the bed and counted all the dimes I had. Not enough for a whole day of calls. And I would need to go into town anyway to eat—there was a scrap of a town five minutes back down the road. I pulled my shoes on and went out to the pay phone, happy to be free of the room even for a minute.

Nick picked up on the third ring. I was so happy to hear his voice I almost dropped the receiver. He had a staff job now, reporting for the *Times*, but he'd been a stringer when I met him three years ago. I was on a job in Santo Domingo, and so was he. We were staying in the same hotel and became friendly. My job went badly, I was backed into a dangerous spot, and he was the only one on the island I could call when it happened although he was little more than an acquaintance at the time. He came when I needed him and probably saved me from prison. I held a great and revolving debt to him. I fed him tips sometimes from my own work, hoping to service this debt, although it did not compare. Mostly Max and I just loved him. We dragged him to our house on weekends and fed him huge meals.

"Good morning," I said. "I'm on a pay phone and it's long distance so I have to talk fast."

"Vera?" he said. "Is that you? Of course it's you."

"I'm in California," I said. I told him what had happened.

"A hospital?" he said.

"That's what they said. She spelled out the name for them. But that was it."

"Why would she run off like that?" he said.

"I don't know," I said. "She was upset. It's very strange here. Aloysius—her father—her whole family—I don't have time. I don't have enough change."

"Mineral Springs," he said. "No city."

"No city. But she would have started in Bel Air."

"And drove north?"

"I have no idea."

He sighed, and then he was quiet for a minute, thinking. "Medical directory," he said finally. "The boards keep directories. The college of surgeons, the college of this and that."

"Can you get one?"

"I think so," he said. "They've got a pile of them in the medical library at NYU."

"I wouldn't ask if it wasn't important," I said.

"You don't have to explain," he said, laughing. "You're always explaining."

I gave him the number of the pay phone and told him I would try him again in a few hours if I didn't hear. Then I called my service. There were two work messages, nothing from Max. I hadn't realized how much I had been hoping until my hopes were disappointed. I went to the car and got the road atlas, and then stood at the pay phone for a while, propping the book open against the glass wall of the booth, running my finger along the 101.

"Mineral Springs Hospital, please."

"What city?"

"Los Angeles."

"I'm afraid there's nothing listed by that name."

"Calabasas."

"No listing."

"Thousand Oaks."

"No listing."

"Camarillo."

"No listing."

"Ventura."

"No listing."

This went on for a while. Eventually my interlocutor said, "Ma'am—"

"It's not a joke," I said quickly. "I'm not having fun with you."

"Of course, ma'am. Maybe you got the name of the hospital wrong," she said gently.

"Maybe," I said. "Two more?"

"Certainly, ma'am."

By this time, I had moved on to other highways and other cardinal directions. I was somewhere in Orange County. "Irvine," I said.

"No listing."

"Lake Forest."

"No listing."

"Okay," I said, feeling heavy and hopeless. "Thank you."

"You're very welcome."

I hung up the phone. An old man stepped out of a room down the concrete walk and stood blinking in the silver light, a towel around his neck. A woman was pushing a cleaning cart over from the office. The moment was hemmed in with a disoriented despair that I had felt before—always on jobs. The feeling that comes with washing up in a distant place and not knowing how to get back or even how to explain having arrived. Being marooned.

I went back into the motel room to wash my face and then drove back down the road to the town I had come through the night before, where there was a Howard Johnson's beside a single-story elementary school and a dusty pink boutique with a sign that read SOMETHING FOR LADIES. The Howard Johnson's gladdened my heart. A couple of tractor trailers were parked in the lot, and an assortment of smaller vehicles, but even this crowded scene did little to beat back the silence of the mountains. Inside, however, there were the busy noises I had hoped for—the clatter of dishes through the swinging kitchen doors, men talking at the counter, the Jackson Five coming at a polite volume through overhead speakers. I asked for a table near the front so I could keep an eye on the highway and the car. I ordered an omelet and coffee and read the libretto while I waited for it to come.

Aimee sat stage right in the bar in Mexico. At center stage, a mezzo-soprano sang the news.

McPherson presumed drowned
Disappeared while swimming
At Venice Beach

Then a chorus of parishioners, who gathered at the back of the stage:

Sister Aimee is with Jesus
Pray for her
Sister Aimee is with Jesus
Pray for her

The notation had it repeat many times, an unspecified number of times. Downstage, her teenage children stood with their arms around each other.

I was crying. I was not a superstitious person, but it was difficult to read about this grief in this particular moment, in this Howard Johnson's on the dry flank of a mountain in San Luis Obispo County. And it made me wonder—a helpless disloyalty, coming from the most forlorn and childlike part of my mind, the part that stood with the two figures at the edge of the stage, staring out into the theater—if this was some sign that Max had been dreaming of running away long before she drove off on Tuesday morning. An unanswerable question that helped me not at all. I closed the libretto and sat for a few minutes drinking my coffee, looking out at the innocent blacktop. When we were together again I would—I didn't know. I

wanted some change. I wanted us to hide together in some remote place. I wanted us to live in a forest primeval with a pack
of dogs. But, no—what I wanted, actually, was for Max to be
sitting on the floor in our front room with a half dozen friends,
having a planning committee meeting. She had been hosting
them at our place for the Gay Liberation Front, and she would
sit with her arms around her knees, or stitching a LAVENDER
MENACE banner, or trying to cajole the committee members
into accepting a little brandy in their coffee, while the group
made costumes for street actions and drafted letters to newspapers. She had taught me how to join with people. I had never
had the heart for politics before. I was ashamed of what I had
done with the CIA and had too melancholic a character to
think I could do better, or that something better was possible.
Max was not an optimist by nature, but she was not a pessimist
either. She just did not presume to know the future. I had asked
her if she thought these things the GLF wanted could come
to pass—that gay people could live like anybody else, without
secrets or threats. Not just in the Village but everywhere. And
she had said, "Wouldn't it be natural?" I had walked around
for a whole day thinking of that question. Wouldn't it be? If I
looked back through my life, and cut out with scissors all the
times when I had accepted a bad lease or a bad job or some
shoddy treatment from another person because I thought the
alternative would draw too much attention to me, because I
worried that person saw something in me that I was trying
to conceal—I didn't know what shape it might have taken.
And I was happy with my life. I had done well at surviving. I
hadn't felt shame, not within myself, since I was a teenager just

grasping the edges of what made me different. All this hiding had not been for me. It had been for them—for everyone else. What if it hadn't been necessary? Unimaginable world.

Max could imagine it. She wasn't certain it would come, the way some of the women in the group were, but she could picture it. Maybe she just lived with broader possibilities than I did. She had come from another planet, after all. Nick, too, got excited about gay liberation, although he couldn't join the marches; all protests, rallies, and actions were forbidden under the terms of his *Times* contract, which required that staff reporters be "apolitical."

The thing Max had said about my mother two days before still rankled. *If we were in Washington, what would you say to your mother?* What did this new world look like to Elizabeth Kelly? She would have known all about the marches, she was an editor at a news magazine. She and my father had worked against segregation when I was a child. She thought of herself as worldly, sophisticated. Her politics were not conservative, but her personal conduct was. She had managed to work in a job explicitly intended for a man chiefly by being impeccable. She smoothed down any peculiarities and eccentricities that she might once have had. She displayed nothing of her desires or frustrations. She didn't speak about me at work. Some of her colleagues told me, when she brought me once to an office Christmas party when I was sixteen, that they had worked with Liz for years before they knew she was a widow, let alone a mother. I doubted she could understand what gay people were asking for now. She took it for granted that the price of access to society was a rupture, sometimes permanent, between the inner and outer selves. And here were a lot of people—people with uncombed hair and no support garments on, no less—demanding access for their whole selves.

When I was seventeen, I took my mother's car after an argument and drove to see a sympathetic aunt in Baltimore, and my mother reported it stolen and had me arrested. I spent thirty days in juvenile detention. Afterward she sent me to a boarding school for affluent delinquents, where I finished my education. She did not attend my graduation, and shortly afterward I moved up to New York and we didn't speak for two years. I didn't see her again in person until I was twenty-six. We'd had a couple of visits in the years since. There were so few things we could talk about—politics, the war. When she was at loose ends for conversation, she resorted to lists of weddings and births among my old classmates from Bethesda-Chevy Chase, the school I had attended before my adjudication. She must have gleaned this information from the alumni newsletter that came to the house. I sometimes thought she knew about me. That fight when I was seventeen had come a few weeks after she had forbidden me from seeing my best friend, Joanne; we had been caught drinking schnapps together. I thought that even Elizabeth Kelly must have been able to see my desperation on being separated from Joanne, my immediate descent into a black pit, for what it was. And now—she asked on our occasional phone calls if I was seeing anyone, but the question had a ritualistic feeling, like the four questions the youngest child asks at Passover. When I told her that Max had moved in with me, she said, "So you're not paying for that house all by yourself." I couldn't tell if this was an attempt to probe or to reassure herself that Max was a roommate I was taking in to economize, so I said nothing. I didn't need her approval. I'd never had it.

And yet, didn't I flinch from the idea of her meeting Max? Was I really free of my old, cowed position if it still hurt to imagine her response?

My breakfast arrived. I was very hungry. I ate quickly, turning the pages of the libretto. Aimee hadn't drowned, of course. She was hiding in Carmel with her married lover. She was jubilant and grandiose. Then they fought, the idyll was over. She had an aria to sing about it. She came back to herself. *I've been mad / or dreaming.* She had to find a way to return to her life. She stood in a red light, begging her children for forgiveness in absentia. She drove south until she was in Mexico. She sat in that bar just over the border, her hands shaking, thinking up a way to resurrect herself.

I was hunched over the plate, looking vaguely out through the front windows at the highway, when a state patrol car pulled into the parking lot.

I sat up and pressed a napkin to my lips. I had parked the Avanti at the end of the lot, between two big trucks, hoping it would go unnoticed there. The cops parked directly in front of the restaurant. I thought their view of the car was obstructed, but I couldn't be sure. My waitress passed by and I waved her down. "Just the check, when you get a minute," I said.

She glanced at my plate. "Everything okay?"

"Delicious."

The waitress had left the water station, but now she was talking to a table of blonde women on the far side of the restaurant. She was the only one on. The whole place was her section. Had I counted up the cost of the meal right? Maybe I could just go. But if they thought I was skipping out on the check and ran after me—well, I could tap her on the shoulder as I left and tell her I'd left the money on the table. But even that would make me look like I was in a rush.

"I'll bring it," she said. She walked away. Two cops got out of the patrol car. One stretched while the other spat on the ground. I watched them walk to the doors and then heard their voices as they came into the carpeted vestibule. The waitress was on the other side of the room at a water station, scribbling on a pad, probably adding up my check. I got my wallet from my purse and counted out the cost of the omelet and coffee, plus tax— was it seven percent? Eight percent?—and tip. I added another dollar in case I was wrong about the tax. The cops had flagged down a girl busing tables, and she was pointing to an empty table in the section I was sitting in.

I was holding the money, but now I set it on the table and took out the libretto again, trying to look relaxed. The police settled into their table. They were no more than fifteen feet from me. They could be anybody, I said to myself, coming from anywhere. There was no reason to think they had anything to do with me at all. They were California Highway Patrol. They probably came through this restaurant every day. But if there was an APB out for a stolen car—and the Avanti was the kind of car that men like that would notice, even if they weren't looking for it—

I stretched my legs under the table and flexed my toes. What I needed to do was calm down. I stared blurrily down at the libretto. I had skipped forward a few pages by accident. Aimee was lying in a hospital bed, surrounded by reporters asking where she had been. Three people had approached her at the beach, she said. *They told me their child was sick.* She claimed she followed them to their car and they chloroformed her.

The waitress with my check stopped to serve the police, who ordered very slowly, with many questions and substitutions. I kept my eyes down and listened, reading two lines on the page again and again. *I was held in a shack in the desert. / I cut the ropes and walked twenty miles.*

"There's onions in the potatoes?" said one cop.

The waitress affirmed this.

"Could I get them without onions?"

She equivocated.

"Never mind, toast," the cop said.

I walked like Moses with his people. / Angels visited me.

"Is it too early for lunch?" said the other cop.

"It is, yeah," said the waitress wearily.

They told me of great things to come.

"Fine," he said. "The eggs and hash."

The waitress, finally released, walked to my table and dropped the check. I passed her the money and thanked her, pushing my things into my bag. "Thanks," she said, but I was already halfway to the door.

I drove back down the road to the motel and gathered my things from the bed and floor of my room in two minutes, cursing the casual way I had thrown them around, as if I were on vacation. I had grown careless in the last few years. It had been a while since anybody was after me. I hurried across to the office and settled the bill with the day clerk, a gleaming thirtyish woman with her hair in waves that fanned back from her face. The day was bright and cool. I threw my luggage into the Avanti and did a three-point turn out of the lot. Once on the highway, I briefly allowed myself the catharsis of topping out the speedometer.

CHAPTER 9

I stopped for gas in a valley where hand-painted signs along the road offered honey, goats' milk, and fresh eggs. The attendant gave me directions to the nearest hotel, which was some miles away, and I stopped at the pay phone beside the air machine before getting back in the car. I called Nick, but he didn't pick up. I called my service. There were no new messages.

The hotel I had been directed to was in a small town that crowded an old two-lane highway and faded quickly into nothing on either side. Each storefront had an overhanging wooden sign. The sun was blinding, there was no shade, and when I got out of the car I heard nothing but the curious *pop-pop-pop* of ravens. The hotel was at one end of town, opposite a feedstore that, on closer inspection, turned out to be a souvenir shop with a feedstore theme. The hotel's painted sign read DE LA CORTE in cursive. I checked in. It was more than I would have liked to pay, but I didn't want to spend more time on the road than I needed to that day. The room was in the front, looking over the street, and smelled like dust mites. I dropped my things, opened the curtains and windows, and went down to find a place to stow the car, eventually parking it on a side street next to a defunct parking meter.

There was a pay phone in front of a grocery store, and I tried my luck with information again.

"Mineral Springs Hospital."

"What city, ma'am?"

"Oceanside."

"No listing, ma'am."

"Try Carlsbad."

"No listing, ma'am."

"Encinitas."

"No listing."

"Solana Beach."

"No listing."

"Del Mar."

"No listing."

I had so little to go on. It was difficult to maintain the hope that I could fix this. I tried Nick again—still nothing. I banged the phone into the cradle, then walked to the hotel and sat on a bench in front, not wanting to go up to the room, which was filled with pink details that irritated me—the toilet paper and tissues under crocheted covers, the dishes of potpourri on the dresser and bedside table and the back of the trickling toilet. The fresh air was nice. I took the libretto out of my bag.

Aimee's story was under suspicion. She was arrested, then released on bond. Preparations for a trial dragged on. She was the butt of jokes. Her mother appeared upstage to urge her on to bigger and grander performances and revivals—her people still loved her. Aimee sang, *I need a place to rest / And get back my health.*

And her mother, out of the darkness upstage, sang, *Ask the oilman again.*

Aimee said, *I could build a place to take the waters.*

I paused on this. A car was going very slowly down the street, the windows down, a teenager at the wheel. A rock song I didn't recognize was playing on the radio. I was excited. Was it something? My hopes attached to this small idea. Was she writing about McPherson building a hospital with Comstock money? A hospital on a mineral spring?

I went back to the pay phone and called Nick again. This time he picked up.

"They wouldn't let me in," he said, breathless. "I've never had a problem before. Today they wanted identification. They said it was students only. Well, of course it is. But they never asked before."

"Could it be a Comstock hospital?" I said.

"Where Max is? Do they have hospitals?"

"I have something with me that Max is writing," I said. "What if they financed a hospital, once upon a time?"

"What does it say?"

"Well—" My loyalty, belatedly, surged up to protect her project. I decided to elide the details, as if I were concealing the identity of a minor. "Well, it's about a woman in the 1920s going through all kinds of things, but at one point she asks the Comstocks for money to build a church, which did happen, Max told me about it once, and then later, she says she needs to rest and 'take the waters,' and she's going to ask the Comstocks for money again."

"The waters?"

"Right. Did the Comstocks ever build a hospital?"

"I think I could find out," he said. "I could make some calls. They've got a foundation."

"Thank you, thank you," I said.

He clicked off. I faced the empty, blazing afternoon. Too restless to stay on the bench, I walked down to a tiny library branch, attached to a post office, that I had seen while I was parking the car. There was no one in it but a wizened woman smoking at the reference desk. Casement windows stood open, and the dry valley air lifted the edges of the flyers and notices pinned to a bulletin board. I asked for the yellow pages and looked through it for a while, not hoping for much and not finding anything.

✦

"It's a private sanatorium," Nick said. "Mineral Springs Hospital, 2500 Kestrel Road, Artemisa, California. Only seventy-five beds."

"But that doesn't make any sense," I said, leaning into the pay phone. "Why would she be in a sanatorium?"

"I don't know, love. I wrote it down. I talked to somebody at the foundation, I told them I was writing a piece. 'Mineral Springs Hospital, endowed by Clara P. and John F. Comstock in 1927.' Aloysius sits on the board."

"Oh," I said, a syllable like a coal chute, straight down.

"What are you going to do?"

"He was lying to me," I said to the vacant street. "He told me she just drove away."

"You think he's involved in this?" Nick said.

"Of course he is." In my mind's eye I saw St. James again as well, saw the two of them conferring. And Max, walking down the steep hill in the morning sun, while I lay sleeping in our bed. "He must have had her committed." She must have been afraid. And I had been nearby and useless.

Nick said, "That happened to an old boyfriend of mine when he was sixteen. His father caught him with another boy, and they sent him to a state hospital. He nearly killed himself trying to get out of there."

"I think they've told the police that I stole her car," I said. "I've been looking over my shoulder since I left. If I get arrested on the way, I don't have anyone out here to post bond."

"On the way? What are you going to do?"

"I'm going to go get her."

There was a pause. "Right," he said. "I wish I was there. I wish I could help."

"You're more use to me at home," I said.

⊕

I had been driving the wrong way all along. Artemisa was a dot on the map seventy miles south of Los Angeles, in the San Gabriel Mountains, not far from the coast. It would be night by the time I got there. I found the woman who ran the hotel, who was confused that I was checking out, since I had just arrived. She asked me several times if anything was wrong and then insisted on returning the money I had paid for the room, for which I thanked her. I took my things back down to the street and retrieved the car. In its brief time at the broken parking meter, a thin film of dust had already settled over the gleaming silvery paint.

On the drive south I thought of many different ways I could breach the sanatorium, people I could claim to be and business I could pretend to be on. But all the time, I knew there was only one thing that was likely to work. It raised goose bumps down my arms. But there it was.

I stopped to stretch my legs and use a bathroom at a restaurant in Gaviota and called Nick again.

"I have to check myself in, don't I?" I said.

There was a pause on the line. "I think so, probably," he said finally. "It's private—it's unlisted. They're not going to let you in if you're not a patient."

"They're going to want to know who's paying for it, then," I said.

"Ah, is there a bit of acting in it for me?" Nick said, trying to sound cheerful. "Who am I? A wealthy boyfriend? A wealthy brother? A wealthy, young, vivacious uncle?"

"Brother," I said. "You're very worried about me."

"What have you been up to?"

"Oh, I've been drinking and taking pills and behaving erratically in nightclubs."

"It's been in all the papers," Nick agreed.

"The East Coast papers."

"Yes, only the East Coast papers. What's my name?"

"Nick Kelly, of course."

"Of course."

"I'll have to use my own name," I said. "The only ID I have on me is my real one."

"All right," he said. "I'll call now so they'll be expecting you."

⊕

I reached Los Angeles in the dark, the tract houses reappearing. The sky was dusky orange. I had thought the freeway might take me around the city, but I realized now that there was no avoiding Los Angeles, not really. It had no edges. Traffic slowed halfway through, or what the map indicated was halfway through. I was disoriented, but sometimes I caught glimpses of skyscrapers that must have been downtown. I straggled out long after rush hour. Many hours of driving were beginning to affect my mind. At home, I was rarely on the road for more than an hour or so, and my old Chevy spent weeks at a time in a garage spot I paid for in a semiformal arrangement with a produce wholesaler in Flatbush. When I glanced in the rearview mirror, I saw that I had the surprised expression of a person keeping her eyes open by force of her eyebrows. It had been a long day.

South of Los Angeles I missed an exit and spent twenty minutes circling in a subdivision, the houses nearly all unlit, the bright sky heavy overhead. Finally I gave up, defeated by the lack of signs, and stopped to look at the map. I turned the dome light on and lowered the window. The night air smelled sweet. The engine ticked. I had been driving for four hours by then, and it was just after nine o'clock in the evening. It was a warm night, and a television was playing just inside a screened window in the house closest to the curb where I sat. I could hear laughter and unintelligible voices, and beyond that, no other sounds but the faint hum of the freeway I could not locate.

She had to know I was coming for her. I couldn't stand to think of her there, lying on a thin and crackling institutional mattress in some ward, not knowing if I had gotten her message or understood it, or if I would be able to fill in the parts that were missing. She must have been interrupted, making the call, or she would have said more. I had never been in a ward, but I had been in juvie and I had friends who had been put away. I had heard awful stories, like Nick had. This place could not be as bad as that, I told myself—it wasn't Bellevue. It was private and small. Maybe the kind of place where the studios used to send actors to dry out. Or maybe they had filled her with Thorazine and beaten her up. I put my hands to my face to calm down. My fingers were cold.

I found my spot on the map and traced the route back to the freeway once, twice, three times, but then I sat for a few more minutes, preparing myself for the drive. Once I was in the sanatorium—if I succeeded in getting in—it would not be simple to get out, and I was afraid. They were very free with injectable sedatives and four-point restraints in places like that, my friends had said. It was routine to be pinned and sedated. It was routine to turn up on visiting days with thumb-sized bruises up and down your arms or be denied visiting days entirely. I turned the key and put the car in first. I found my way back to the freeway.

Around ten I finally turned off onto Kestrel Road, which led away from the busy flats and up into the mountains. I passed a few small white houses, and then nothing at all for a while. I came to a T-junction that I knew meant I had gone too far. I made a three-point turn, surprising some glowing-eyed small animal in the dark, and retraced the route more slowly, peering at the margin of the road. This time I saw the sign, half-hidden in the scrub: MINERAL SPRINGS HOSPITAL—PRIVATE DRIVE.

I rolled to a stop. I hadn't seen another car in twenty minutes. I thought through my options and decided not to present myself now, so late at night. They might not even accept new patients at this hour. Anyway, I needed to eat and sleep before I could work up the nerve to bluster through a psychiatric intake.

I drove back down the mountain and found a McDonald's, and then sat eating in the parking lot with the windows down, listening to the traffic, watching the lights blinking in the dark hills. I was getting low on money and was too tired to navigate any further that night. I pushed my seat back as far as it would go and fell asleep.

⊕

The rising sun woke me at six o'clock. My neck and shoulder ached. Thirty was too old to be sleeping in cars. I turned on my side and raised my head over the windowsill. Butter-yellow light flooded the empty McDonald's parking lot. I would see her today.

I had a foul taste in my mouth, and my hair was matted. I winced when I moved. But maybe all this would help with my clinical presentation. I got out, gathering some dimes from the bottom of my purse, and went in for a cup of coffee.

⊕

I found the turnoff with less difficulty in daylight. The sign was half-screened by a bush, as I remembered. There were few trees on the mountain—mostly dry grasses and low shrubbery, tough dusty flora. The sky was cloudless and immense, and I felt both exposed and profoundly unwitnessed as I drove in the little car. I went through a pass, and from there the road descended and I could see the sanatorium, set in a cleft in the slope, hanging above a dry valley, as if it had been falling and had caught there.

My palms started to sweat. As often happened when I was frightened, my vision sharpened, which made small things at the corners of my eyes distinct enough to distract me. At the last turn before the road ended in a concrete parking lot, I braked as something dark darted across my path, and then saw that it was the shadow of a hawk. I pulled into the lot and hummed to myself for a couple of minutes, a habit that some-times helped but, in this case, did not.

The sanatorium was a whitewashed, mission-style building, its rows of windows very dark in the bright morning. The park-ing lot was slightly above and behind it, so I approached from a vantage point that let me look down onto the orange tiles of the roof, which had a bell tower at one end. Outcroppings of glittering rock and the sound of water running in the valley sug-gested the location of the mineral springs. The gravel path sloped sharply downward and left me in front of a large portico. I stood there for a minute, combing my hair with my fingers. In the shadow of the portico was a set of glass doors, incongruous in this architecture, like the entrance to a supermarket.

I walked into an entrance hall, carrying my suitcase and handbag. A nurse sat behind an ornate reception desk. I was overwhelmed by a dim, tiled hush.

"Can I help you?" said the nurse.

"Yes," I said. "I've come—I wanted to—"

She looked down at something hidden from me by the ledge of the desk. "Are you Miss Kelly?"

It was so strange to hear my real name. I had a cache of fake documents at home, with two different aliases—Rose Davies and Anne Patterson, with their slightly variant dates of birth, cities of origin, travel histories and restrictions. But those were for work, and I hadn't thought I was working when I came to California. I was only myself. "Yes," I said.

"We expected you last night," she said.

"I arrived late," I said. "I'm sorry."

"Well, Dr. Clark may be able to see you soon anyway for intake," she said. "Before morning rounds." She stood and walked away down the hall, and after a beat or two I followed, although she didn't make any indication that I should. She stopped at a door and turned to watch me approach. Some old part of me was surfacing, the institutionalized part: slow-moving, resistant, avoidant.

"Wait here with Miss Baumgarten," she said.

Through the doorway was a windowless secretarial anteroom, where Miss Baumgarten, an older woman with hair dyed red-orange, was ripping a packet of Alka-Seltzer open over a glass of water. "Morning," she said to the nurse. Behind her, a doorway opened into a carpeted office, with a nameplate that said DR. CLARK—HEAD PSYCHIATRIST.

The nurse left. Miss Baumgarten maintained her focus on the fizzing glass of water. There was a chair on my side of the desk. After a minute I sat in it.

"He's not in yet?" I said, nodding to the psychiatrist's office.

She lifted her head and peered at me. On her desk, a ceramic figure of a book, held open by an undersized ceramic angel, displayed the words THIS IS THE DAY THE LORD HATH MADE; REJOICE AND BE GLAD IN IT.

"He's not in yet," she said, with such a perfect lack of tone that I couldn't be sure if she was repeating my question back to me.

Time passed. I couldn't see a clock. There was little to hear but the squeak of nurses' shoes in the hall. After a while, a man with a large bald head came in, nodded to Miss Baumgarten, and went through into the bigger office. "Who is that, Miss Baumgarten?" he called over his shoulder.

"The intake from last night," she said.

"Send her in in five minutes," he said.

Miss Baumgarten rifled through a handbag for a while and then said, "You can go in now."

I could see that the office was meant to be impressive. There was a lot of extraneous furniture. The carpet was so new it still had its chemical smell. His windows gave a panorama of the mountain. A couple of expensive-looking pens stood upright in a ceramic hedgehog on his desk. They were supposed to look like quills, but the effect was more like a bull in a bullfight, trailing the pikes of the picadors.

"You were expected last night," he said. "But I suppose I'll do the intake now."

"Thank you," I said.

"Drugs," he said.

He had patchy eyebrows, which he raised.

"Yes," I said. "Yes, that's—it's been a problem."

"What do you have with you?"

"I didn't bring anything with me," I said. For a second I felt like a dinner party guest who had forgotten to bring a bottle of wine.

"Our policies are very clear," he said. "There's no amnesty past this room. If you have drugs with you, you give them up now. After this point, you'll be searched, and what we find then, we'll call the police about. So this is your only chance."

"I don't have anything," I repeated.

"Hm," he said. He took a packet of papers from a drawer and sifted through them, making notes. "Why are you here, Miss Kelly?"

He was backlit by the glowing mountain. I looked at the ceiling.

"I haven't been feeling good," I said. "My family is upset about the pills."

"What have you been taking?"

"A lot of things. Quaaludes, Valium, amphetamines."

"When did it start?"

"My doctor prescribed me some things a few years ago when I was—I had bad nerves."

He looked at me without responding, so I improvised for a while. I had bad nerves because my mother was stifling and critical. My father was dead. I wanted to be thin like the other girls. I had a fiancé who threw me over. I let money hum through

135

the whole story—a series of breakdowns at beach houses in East Hampton, at charity galas, on capricious vacations. My family had extended my trust, declared me incompetent. My brother held the purse strings. They might hand it over if I cleaned up.

Dr. Clark took notes while I talked and interjected now and then to ask invasive questions. He wanted to know when I'd had my first period. Whether I was having sex with the now-irrelevant fiancé and, if so, how often. What my nightmares were like. This is my nightmare, I thought. This sticky, affectless probing. It was all lies, but I had chosen lies with some relation to the truth, because they were easier to remember and enact, and even this adjacent contact with my real life made me want to run away and hide.

After forty-five minutes he said, "Miss Kelly, do you want to get well?"

I wanted to roll down the mountain and lie in the springs until it got dark. Was that the same thing? "Yes," I said.

"Then you follow the program," he said.

"Okay."

He creaked thoughtfully in his chair. "You follow the program," he said again.

When I was seventeen and went to juvenile detention, they took away everything I came in with. It was a chilly, hateful ritual in a small room off the main hall. I had to strip and empty my pockets, and a woman watched me do it and then pushed everything into a paper bag and wordlessly handed me a uniform to wear, which was too tight under the arms and too thin for the weather. I had spoken to other girls afterward and they had confirmed that it was always the same. Nobody got to change alone, and they never told anybody what they were going to do with our things. I suppose they sent mine to my mother. I never got them back from her. Where was the trivial stuff I'd had in my pockets that day, the last day that I was a child who lived at home? Was it still in a drawer somewhere in the brick house in Chevy Chase?

At Mineral Springs I was allowed to change alone. I stood in a room with two single beds and two plastic chests of drawers while a nurse waited outside the door. I pulled off my dress, which was crumpled from being slept in and smelled like me, and nudged my shoes off my feet. The uniform was cream-colored, limp and fuzzed on the surface from many washings, a shapeless top and pants like surgical scrubs. I had also been given slippers. I looked at the slippers on the floor next to my own shoes for a long time. My shoes, which I had bought in a shop on Seventh Avenue one afternoon just after Christmas, and which Max had liked, and which were covered in dust from where I'd been.

I could not feel Max's presence. Had I expected to? I put on the exhausted cotton top, pulled up the elastic waistband of the pants. She was here; she had to be here. She was close by. I took the key to the Avanti off its ring and slipped it into my bra, along with the money I had left and my driver's license. Then I put the empty wallet back in my purse and dropped the purse into the bag I had been given for all my belongings.

Once I had changed, the nurse came in and took the bag and my suitcase away, then returned for me. She told me that lunch would be served at eleven thirty, and then led me on a tour of the ward. "It's almost nine anyway," she said. "Which is first rounds." As we passed each door, she turned the handle and pushed it in. The doors swung and rebounded. In most rooms, limp figures stirred under white blankets at this intrusion, and once or twice the opening door revealed a patient sitting up in bed or standing at the window in a robe. My heart seized each time, thinking that I saw or was about to see Max's face. "This is the voluntary ward," said the nurse. "Involuntary is further down, we're not going there. You start out in a double room. If you make progress, you get a single."

"Progress?" I said.

"If your attendance at group is good. If you come to meals. No fights. Group is at ten and three."

The floors were tiled in dark blue. The walls were painted halfway up in the same color but then changed to cream. Through a doorway I could see a courtyard done in figured Spanish tile, with large empty planters around a dry fountain. Deck chairs were lined up haphazardly down the middle of it, where the sun fell. It needed sweeping. The nurse saw me looking. "Voluntary patients get patio time," she said. "Involuntary patients have to smoke in the lounge." We paused at a doorway with no door in it. "This is the lounge."

So this was a place where the two sides mixed. It was empty. Rows of new chairs and a couple of love seats faced a large television. There was an Ansel Adams print on the wall. The place had the look of a showpiece, somewhere visitors might come. Plumy ferns enlivened the corners. There were clean ashtrays everywhere.

"Time in the lounge is a privilege," said the nurse.

It was making me claustrophobic, standing here and looking at a stack of battered board games on a table. The words *occupational therapy* drifted down to me through the years. The tedium of confinement and the insult of the ways we were expected to spend our time. They made us knit and crochet and memorize food safety information. Board games had been reserved for Friday nights, and if we misbehaved, our access to the closet where the games were kept was suspended. The girls who had lost their privileges sat furiously in silence on Friday nights, or picked fights to amuse themselves.

"Can we go outside?" I said.

"Voluntary patients can go outside," she said.

"How often?"

She looked at me as if I had said something funny. "Why don't you settle in first," she said.

She led me back down the hall, past a telephone in an alcove beside the nurses' station. "Voluntary patients may use the telephone once per day," she said. "Five minutes maximum. Sign in with a nurse." She stopped in a doorway. "This one is yours. Claire, you've got a roommate."

There was one empty bed and one occupied by Claire, who was a tremendous riot of blonde hair and an eyeshade. She turned blindly toward the door as I came in and frowned.

"Lunch is at eleven thirty," the nurse said again, and left.

I sat on the empty bed. Claire turned away and pulled the white blanket up again. A precarious silence spread. The blinds were down, and after a minute I stood and raised them, reasoning that she wouldn't notice. The window faced down the slope in front of the hospital, and the midmorning sun blazed down. I could see water running in the valley below, pooling among boulders. In the distance, the endless suburbs lay under haze.

I could sleep for a few minutes. What was the harm? I could see already that the one thing that abounded here was time. I lay down and let my slippers drop off my feet. After a night folded up in the car, the hard mattress was consoling to my back.

CHAPTER 10

Claire was standing over me, smoking.

"Hello?" I croaked.

She leaned toward the window, which she had opened an inch, as far as it would go, and ashed the cigarette into the empty sunshine.

"I've had this room to myself," she said.

"What time is it?" I said.

"Are you noisy?" she said. "Are you a noisy person?"

I sat up, becoming aware again of the institutional pajamas I was wearing. "I don't think so."

"What's the point of trying to get better if you can't sleep, can't rest, can't be alone?"

She had tucked her top into her elastic waistband and rolled up the legs of the pants, creating a kind of capri silhouette, like Audrey Hepburn in an insane asylum. She seemed to expect an answer from me.

"You can't sleep?" I said.

"All I fucking do is lie in bed and not sleep," she said.

"Are you allowed to smoke in here?" I said.

"No," she said. She walked to her own bed, then turned and came back. "So I guess you're going to be hostile."

"What?"

"About the cigarettes."

"No, I'm not going to be hostile about the cigarettes."

She hesitated. "Do you want one?"

I laughed. "I quit, thanks."

"If you tell the nurse about the cigarettes, I'll tell her we were both doing it."

"Fine." I wished I had a mirror. I was disoriented. My head hurt.

"It's lunch," Claire said.

"Oh." I squinted at her. "Okay, thanks."

She turned abruptly and walked out. I listened to the irritated slap of her feet fading down the hall, and then followed her. Two women stood out there, patients, arrested in motion fifteen feet apart, as if they had been on some urgent business but had forgotten what it was. One was grinding her teeth. A nurse at the nurses' station ignored them both. The dining room was down a side hall, and I caught up with Claire standing in the doorway, waiting for a knot of women to clear out of her way, shaking her hands and hissing, "Go, go, *goooo.*"

"I'm hungry," I said out loud to no one in particular.

The blockade cleared and Claire buttonhooked furiously toward a table in the far corner. The tables were covered with a heavy plastic fabric in mauve, and a bud vase on each one held an artificial stalk of lily of the valley. I followed her. She didn't like me, but at least we were acquainted. She glanced up when

I sat down but said nothing. Staff in hairnets were circling the room, pushing trolleys loaded with trays.

"They try to make this place sound deluxe," Claire said. "But it's the same food everywhere."

"You've been to other places?" I said.

She looked offended. "You haven't?"

"I guess this is my first time."

"You guess?"

"This is my first time."

"Well, hooray for you. Maybe it will stick."

An aide set trays in front of both of us. Claire went to work, with long nervous fingers, on a tiny carton of apple juice. A piece of fish splayed across some rice. "I hate the fish," she said. Then she added, conciliatory, "But it's good for your skin."

I ate fast and looked around the room. It was perhaps half-full. There was little talking. Every patient I'd seen was white. Did they still segregate these places? A couple of women stared toward the windows, sitting upright before untouched plates. The rest slumped over their meals like tents badly staked. "Is this everyone?" I said to Claire.

"No, a lot of people sleep through lunch," she said. "I wish I was on those meds. I've gained six pounds on lithium since I got here."

She had put a headband in her masses of hair. Flecks of mascara clung to her lashes. "Do they let us have makeup in here?" I said.

"Sure, it's not prison."

"Oh. I thought—"

"You have to check it out from the charge nurse, though."

She was young. I would have been surprised if she was more than twenty-three. A pretty, oval face, but a hard tension around the mouth, and all that hair, teased up and sprayed at the crown, a rampart of hair. "Where are you from, Claire?"

"Hollywood."

"Oh?"

"Yeah." She swallowed the apple juice in one go. "This is my third time here. My folks are sentimental about it. I keep telling them it's a dump, but they don't care. I was in Costa Dorada last winter—a million times better than this place. They had a pool and a masseuse." She looked appraisingly at me. "What do they have you on?"

"Nothing."

Her eyebrows went up. "Nothing?"

I shook my head. She seemed interested in me for the first time. "What's the point of putting you on nothing?" Her face cleared. "No, they probably just haven't worked up your scrips yet, since you just got in."

How had I failed to think of this? My heart turned over. "But I don't know if I need anything. I mean"—I had to decide, quickly, whether this was the kind of thing people talked about here or if they kept it to themselves—"pills are my problem in the first place."

"Probably just a sedative, then," she said.

"Why would I need a sedative?"

Her brow wrinkled. "This really is your first time, I guess. How old are you? The ones coming off pills always come unglued. It's easier for the staff to give them sedatives up front."

"I'm thirty," I murmured, picturing myself thrashing while a team of nurses held me down.

"Pah!" She was shocked. I remembered being twenty-three and unable to imagine thirty. She leaned across the table and put the pads of her fingers on the left side of my face. "Good skin, though," she said to herself.

I leaned back, slowly. "Where do the involuntary patients eat?" I said.

"In their rooms, I guess? They give me the creeps." She gathered the various scraps and bits of her meal together into the center of her plate and pushed away from the table. "I'm going back, I want to lie down."

She left me alone with her tray. After a minute I realized I was staring into space.

⊕

On the telephone in the hall, using my allotted five minutes and having been informed that long-distance calls would be added to my fees, I dialed Nick's number.

"Oh God, I'm glad to hear your voice," he said. "I've just been sitting here chewing on my fingers."

"I'm okay," I said. I was always startled by the warmth of other people's worry. "I'm here." I was only a few feet from the nurses' station. "No privacy."

"No, of course. Have you seen her?"

"There are separate sides. Maybe this afternoon."

"I told them I was wiring $600 to them today," he said.

"Did you?" I said, surprised. Nick was always short at the end of the month.

"Did I what?"

"Wire them the money?"

"No, sweetheart, I don't have $600."

"Right," I said, relieved. If he emptied his bank account for us, I didn't know how we would pay him back. "Well, you have our key—the bankbooks are in the left-hand drawer of my desk." There might have been $350 in the account that Max and I shared, and most of it was spent already in our minds, on car repairs for me and new eyeglasses for her—she wore them to read and had lost them in March—and a ground-floor window that I had broken with the end of a ladder I was carrying over my shoulder. But if spending it all kept me in Mineral Springs another day, then I would have to spend it all. There was nothing to think of except today.

"Only if it comes to that," Nick said. "I don't think they'll call me about the money again until tomorrow."

A nurse appeared at my elbow. "Miss Kelly, you're not allowed to use the phone yet," she said.

I pulled away. She was so close to me. "I thought—? They checked it out to me."

"Who did?" She looked past me to the nurses' station, where the young woman who had let me use the telephone was sitting with a stricken face. "She shouldn't have. You haven't been here twenty-four hours yet."

"Sorry, sorry." I hadn't covered the receiver; Nick could hear everything. The nurse reached over me, took the telephone from my hand, and hung it up.

"You should be in your room for medication rounds," she said. "It's 12:25."

"Sorry," I said again, shuffling away backward.

Claire was in there reading a book called *A Gift of Prophecy*. On the cover, a woman in a Lady Bird Johnson bob gazed complacently into a crystal ball. Claire had closed the blinds. I sat on my bed in the semidarkness. The voices of nurses came down the hall, the sound of rapping on doors. The single word *rounds* repeated.

"Do I have to take the meds?" I said.

"Yeah," Claire said, turning the page with a flick of her finger.

"Even though I'm voluntary?"

"Yeah. If you don't take the meds they can discharge you for noncompliance."

"What are yours like?"

She looked up, bored. "I don't know, who knows? They all make you feel like you've got mud for blood."

We waited in silence. The pages of her book rasped.

"Is it good?" I said.

She turned the book around in her hands to look at the cover, as if she had forgotten what it was. "She's psychic," she said. "Important people are always calling her and begging her for help. The president and movie stars and people like that."

"Can I cheek it?" I said. My heart was starting to hammer. I didn't see how I could do what I needed to do if I was full of sedatives.

"You can try. But sometimes they look in your mouth."

"Oh."

"Do you have a phobia or something?" she said. "You could bring it up in group."

A nurse appeared with a cart in the doorway, knocking on the open door. Claire took her medicine, and the nurse came around the bed and gave me a cup of water and a second cup that held two large, white caplets.

"What are these for?" I said.

She glanced at me. "Those are to keep you calm and help you sleep."

"It's the middle of the day."

Her gaze sharpened. "The treatment plan is from Dr. Clark. You can take it up with him if you want."

"No, that's all right." I shouldn't have said anything. If I was planning to cheek the medications, I had no chance now that I had forced her attention and irritated her. I swallowed the two caplets and handed the empty cups back to her.

⊕

There was nothing to do but walk the halls. Past the patients' rooms, past the offices of the assistant director and the head administrator at the end of the ward, the dispensary, the children's visiting room. I stopped there and looked in. Through wired glass, I saw a dollhouse pushed against one wall, with angry strokes of a crayon all across its roof. A shelf of meek dolls, a Felix the Cat clock bug-eyed on the wall. I was starting to feel heavy. The hallway eddied around me when I turned my head. I had chosen not to stay in my room, in my bed, because I didn't want to sleep through the drugs, thinking it would be too much wasted time. But this was like working inside a diving bell. I walked as far as I could, came to a locked door, and looked through. On the other side, patients were lined up at another dispensary window: involuntaries, I thought, having their own med rounds. Max wasn't there. One patient stood with her arms crossed, apparently asleep on her feet, her chin on her chest. Another chewed her lips and hands. My heart, I thought. My heart . . . some distant organ crimped and folded. My fear, my constant companion since I woke up on Tuesday, retreated to an inner horizon and stayed there. The facts of my life wavered just out of reach. I was calm. I was very calm, and though I felt heavy, there was little resistance and no friction to the way I moved, as if I were sinking through a column of water.

I watched the patients take their medications at the dispensary window, and then I watched them disperse. People wandered back and forth. It occurred to me eventually that they could see me, and so could the nurses. This probably happened all the time—moon-eyed, tranquilized women staring through the window. This thought struggled up from the mud and then, exhausted, sank back down into it. Then: What if I wrote a note and pushed it under the door? I didn't have paper or a pen. Were we allowed pens? I saw Claire again, saying, *It's not prison*. I crouched down to stare at the bottom of the door: a little gap, room for a note. I sat on the floor for a while, laboriously thinking it through. A note, a note, a note. What would it say?

A nurse came to the turn in the hallway and said, "No sitting on the floor."

I clambered to my feet and made my way past her. For a moment I had no idea how I could locate my room again, since they all looked the same, but this thought caused no anxiety. The hall slid past. At every second or third door, I remembered to look in and see if Claire was there. Eventually she was.

"Claire," I said. "Do you have paper and a pen?"

"There's a pad in the dresser," she said. "And maybe a pen. They got most of them."

I went in and opened the top drawer of the dresser on my side of the room.

"In *my* dresser," she said.

I circumnavigated our beds and arrived at her dresser. In the top drawer there was a pad and some underthings. In the back, a pen.

"So what did they give you?" she said.

"I don't know."

"What color was it?"

"White."

"Well, that could be anything. But you look zonked."

Her tone was friendly, even gentle. I pulled the pad and paper up from the depths of the drawer and smiled at her. "I hate it," I said sadly.

"For a pillhead," she said, "you don't like pills much."

"No," I agreed. "I don't like pills much."

"You're writing a letter already?"

"Yeah."

"My parents are always on me to write them."

"Did they send you here?" I said.

"Yeah," she said. She was reading a *Ladies' Home Journal*. I watched the white arc of the turning page.

"Then you shouldn't write them," I said. "You should forget about them."

She looked surprised, and then laughed. "Is that right?"

"They can go to hell."

She laughed again and so did I.

"Go to hell, Doug and Evelyn!" she said.

"Go to hell, Liz!" I said. "My father's dead."

"Oh."

I took a sheet of paper from the pad, which was printed with MINERAL SPRINGS across the top, and put it on my own dresser. Across the top I wrote, *MAX*.

"Who are you writing to?" Claire said.

I turned and said, as placid as a cow, "My girlfriend."

I couldn't read her face. It was hard to focus; I didn't care. Who cared? It was a mental institution. I was thirty years old. They could all go to hell.

"You're a lesbian?" said Claire. "I wouldn't have guessed."

"Well," I said. "You should—" I rummaged around in my brain for a riposte. It was something juvenile, something off the old Chevy Chase playground. What was it? "You should get your eyes checked." There it was.

"Man, they tranked you but good," she said. She put the magazine down. "All right, where's your girlfriend? Is she gonna visit? Nobody visits me."

"She's not going to visit," I said. I stared at the paper. What next?

"Why not?" she said.

Underneath *MAX*, I wrote, *I'M HERE*.

"I was seeing a guy last winter when I was in Costa Dorada, and he visited once," she said. "And then never again. He said it was too depressing. And that place had a pool."

"The pool was depressing?" I said. I wrote, *LOOK FOR ME*.

"No, I mean, he thought it was depressing even though it was nice. That place cost, oh my God. I don't even know."

I folded the note in half and stood up.

"Where are you going?" Claire said.

"Walk."

I went back down the hallway, past the offices and the dispensary and the children's visiting room with its furious crayoning, to the locked door to the involuntary ward. No one was around. I crouched and slid the paper under. If a patient finds it, it'll be fine, I thought. Inmates in places like this love gossip, and they love to know things that staff don't. If a nurse finds it instead, then they'll put it right in the trash and then, I don't know. They might give Max a hard time about it. But what would she say? She'd say, "I don't know anything about that," and it would be the truth.

⊕

I went to the lounge. On the way there, I realized that I had brought the pad and pen with me, in my pocket. Maybe Claire needed it for writing letters. And the pen was contraband. I would give it back to her. I remembered and forgot this several times between the nurses' station and the lounge. When I arrived, three women and two men were arranged around the room, distant from each other. All three women were reading the *Ladies' Home Journal*. A stack of them glinted on a windowsill. One of the men was watching television, which was turned to the news. He was a slight blond man with a mustache, and he was tipped to one side in the chilly embrace of a club chair, an unbearably sad expression on his face. The other was a big man with a lot of black hair and a heavy face, who was kneading a ball of modeling clay between his hands. I sat in the nearest chair facing the windows and looked out into the bright day. The warmth of the sun filled the air and covered me, down my lap to my bare ankles and onto the floor. I closed my eyes. Was it always like this? The warm sun? When I opened my eyes again, I was painlessly blinded.

The big man was standing over me. "Do you have a match?"

"Mm," I said. "No, I quit."

He straightened and turned to the other women. "Shirley, do you—"

"Russell, I told you, I only have three and I'm not giving you one."

"Karmically, Shirley, you're a disaster," he said.

"Get one from the nurse," said another woman.

"It's Annette on. She doesn't smoke either," the man said.

"What a liar," said the third woman. Her hair was cut very short, and it stood up in frustrated curls all over her head. "Annette's a fucking liar."

"Ask Bill," someone offered.

"He's asleep."

"Annette's a cunt," said the short-haired woman.

The blond man watching television said, "Why do they even bother reporting the weather?"

"Language. Jesus," said another woman.

The big man dropped into the chair closest to me and rubbed his forehead. I sat up. "Hey," I said to him. "Is anybody here involuntary?"

He leaned forward and showed me the lump of modeling clay. He had shaped it into a duck. I smiled. He squashed it back to nothing.

"Hey," I said, affronted.

"I'll make it again," he said. I watched him. The duck reappeared.

"You're good at that," I said. I remembered my question. "Is anybody here—"

"I am," he said.

"Oh." Maybe I had just been rude. I reared back, slowly, like a duchess in a play.

"I keep getting my discharge date moved back," he said. "Because I don't want to go to group."

"Why don't you want to go?"

"Have you been?" he said.

"No."

"Well, you'll see." He squashed the duck again.

"Listen," I said. "I think somebody I know is over there. On the involuntary side."

"Yeah?"

"Her name is Max. Have you seen her? She has light brown hair, about this long—she's a little shorter than me. Freckles."

"Maybe I have." He squinted. "Is she new?"

"Yes, just a couple of days."

"I think I have."

I heard ringing in my ears. "You have?"

"Yeah, I've seen her. There haven't been that many new people this week. She's in iso."

"Iso?"

"Isolation."

"Why?"

"A lot of the new ones start out in iso. I did."

"How long have you been here?"

He looked at the ceiling, calculating. "Five—six weeks."

"God."

"It's not too bad. I watch too much TV at home."

In my tranquilized state, there was a gnomic depth to these words. *I watch too much TV at home. At home, I watch too much TV.* He was working on the clay again. "What do you do here?" I said.

"I do some thinking," he said. "I read. I always have somebody bring me some big goddamn books."

"What are you reading?" I said.

"*The Guns of August.*"

"Learned anything?"

He set the ball of clay on a side table. It was a rabbit now. "Things could always be worse."

A small woman with a pixie cut shuffled into the room on slippers that were crushed at the back. Alarm bells rang distantly in my mind. A few seconds went by before I understood the reason. She held a sheet of notepaper in her hand.

"Is there a Max in here?" she said.

I watched with dismay but no fear. I thought, Later on I'm going to think this was pretty stupid.

The man with the clay was staring at me. The small woman held the note up. "It says, 'Max, I'm here, look for me.'"

"There's no Max in here," said Shirley. "Just Russell and Steve."

Russell focused on his rabbit. The small woman stood in the doorway for a minute, scrutinizing the note, its six stupid words. Then she folded it, put it in her pocket, and walked out. From down the hall I heard her say, "Anybody know a Max?"

Russell stood up and casually left the lounge. I waited and then went after him. I found him halfway down the hall, studying a water fountain.

"Well," I said.

"None of my business," he said.

"I appreciate that."

A nurse passed us. "Group is in five," she said.

"Thanks, Annette," said Russell.

"I know you're not going to go," said the nurse. "But you could have a good influence on our newcomer here."

I waited until she was gone and then said, "When are they going to let me go outside?"

"When did you get here?" said Russell.

"This morning."

"Probably tomorrow, then," he said.

I thought, He already knows I'm up to something and he didn't say a word. He can go back and forth between the two sides. Keep going. "She shouldn't be here," I said. "Her father committed her."

"Okay," he said. He backed up politely, as if making room for me in an elevator.

"I don't want to bother you," I said.

"It's fine." He took another step back.

"I'm Vera," I said. I offered my hand. He took it and squeezed it once.

We looked at our shoes. "Do they let us in the mineral springs?" I said finally. "The water?"

"No, no," he said. "They're afraid we'll drown ourselves."

"Well," I said. "It was nice to meet you."

"Likewise."

The nurse passed by again. "Miss Kelly, do you need me to walk you to group?"

I received this as a command and stared helplessly at Russell. "No," I said, then, realizing I didn't know where it was held, "Yes."

"This way."

Russell mustered a little wave. I followed the nurse down the hall. It was difficult to walk in a straight line. I tacked, like a sailboat. She didn't look back. Around a corner she directed me into the dining room. Several tables had been cleared out of the middle, and an ominous ring of chairs filled the space that was left. A game show played on the television in the corner, and six or seven people in pajamas sat in the circle, along with a young woman with her hair in twin braids, who waved a clipboard at me excitedly.

"A newcomer!" she said. "Please sign in! So happy to see you."

The medication relieved me of the burden of choosing an expression. I felt slack, not just in my face but in my arms and legs, my skin. I took the clipboard and wrote my name very slowly. *Vera Kelly*, the *y* trailing off. It was still strange to see it and answer to it in a place like this. My real name. I went back and wrote in my middle initial, a *T.* that I traced over several times, the pen failing, until it was embossed in the paper with its little period.

"Take a seat," said the woman with the braids, who was wearing a name badge on a lanyard. I sat close to her so I could read it and then regretted the choice. The woman at her right hand strained with eagerness to begin, while the people in the more distant chairs in the circle held back, arms crossed, and I thought I belonged with them. The name badge on the lanyard said ALICE COHN—PSYCHIATRY INTERN. "Let's all welcome Vera," she said.

"Welcome, Vera," chorused the group.

"Thank you, doctor," I said.

"Alice," she said.

It was coming back to me—the little office on the second floor of Bethesda-Chevy Chase High School, the smell of floor wax and setting powder. Some flaking Jung paperbacks shelved under an overgrown spider plant. The counselor they had made me talk to after I took a lot of pills at seventeen. She had at least expected me to address her as *Miss*. When did everyone lose their titles? The world swarmed now with undefined professionals. There was always this pressing for intimacy and informality. "Miss Cohn," I murmured.

"Even worse," she said. "Alice."

"She's married," said the eager woman to her right, a redhead with her bangs askew. "She's married to a musician."

"Let's get started," Alice said. "Can we do hands?"

The next person reached across an empty seat and took my hand, and reluctantly I took Alice's, which was small and dry. We sat for a moment quietly, heads bowed, and then Alice said, "All right. Please thank your neighbor for being here."

Around the circle each person turned to one side and said, "Thank you for being here," and then turned to the other side and repeated it. I did this too and then said, to no one in particular, "And also with you."

"Yesterday we had some really good sharing," Alice said. The redhead nodded vigorously. "Let's check in. Dottie, can you start us off?"

The redhead said, "Terrible nightmares all night."

"Tell us about them."

"I was drowning. And then I was on a stage. I was stripped naked. There was an audience and they all turned into bugs."

"Wow," said a small, round man across the circle.

"I shouldn't have had dessert," Dottie said. "Sugar gives me terror."

"Thank you," Alice said. "Frank, can you share?"

Frank said, "This week I'm focused."

"Mm."

"Focused on my health. Keeping my mind clean. I've been doing calisthenics in my room. I do a hundred push-ups by the end of the day."

The small, round man said, "Panting and grunting the whole time."

"Nobody makes you stick around for it," said Frank.

"Jerry," said Alice.

"I'm fine," said the next man. "Pass."

"I want us all to acknowledge that there was a pass," Alice said. "Janet."

"Hopeless," said Janet. "Totally hopeless."

"Can you say more?" said Alice.

"I'm a cow," said Janet. "I'm the size of a house. Even with the Benzedrine." She began to weep. I watched her curiously, but then my attention drifted away. The game show on the television behind me was loud, but also distorted and softened around the edges. The brass-band cadences of the host wouldn't resolve into words. I stared into a tall potted plant in the far corner of the room. That's real, I thought. No—plastic. No—real. Part of it is dead.

It was my turn already. The wide circle had been traversed. Everyone was looking at me. I searched for something to say. "I'm pretty tired."

Alice still looked expectant.

"Very tired," I amended.

"Is that your check-in?" Alice said.

"Oh," I said. "Yes?"

"Maybe you could say more," Alice said. "Newcomers usually say a few words about how they came to be here."

I couldn't remember. I couldn't remember my cover. I blinked hard twice and then put my hand over my eyes.

"It's," I said.

"It's all right," Alice said gently. "Please feel at ease."

"I'm—I couldn't," I said. A blank, blank wall. Say anything at all, I thought.

"I took a lot of pills," I said.

"Mm-hm," said Alice.

"My mother found me," I said, moving forward into the space that was opening up, unsure where I was going. "I took a lot of pills and fell against a fish tank. It smashed and the fish were everywhere." This is fine, I thought, this is fine. Probably as good as the other story.

The small, round man said, as if this were simply too much, "Oh, no."

The house in Chevy Chase. In my memory the rug was still wet when I got home from the hospital, but that couldn't be right. There was no one at home. That was right. There was no one at home. The mess was gone. The house was empty when I came home.

"You're crying," Dottie said loudly. "Thank you."

I touched my face. I was crying. It came as a surprise.

"Good sharing!" Dottie said. She clapped.

"You're welcome," I said.

"Why are you crying?" Alice said.

I squinted at her. How should I know?

"She feels guilty," Jerry said.

I swiveled to look at him. "No," I said.

"Did the fish die?" said Dottie.

"I believe they did," I said.

"I would feel a little guilty," Dottie said.

"Fish," said Frank. "Some fish? That's nothing."

"My mother was upset," I said.

"There you are," said Janet. "She does feel guilty. She's just not in touch with it."

"I'm not in touch with it," I murmured.

"Let's not tell her what she feels," Alice said. "Let her speak."

The circle fell quiet. They were all looking at me.

"Why are you crying?" said Alice again.

A tear rolled over my top lip. I tasted it. "I'm sad," I said.

"Why?" said Alice.

"It's a sad story," I said.

"Why did you take all those pills?" Alice said.

"Were you trying to kill yourself?" said Jerry.

"I don't think so," I said. A burst of celebration came from the television behind me. "I was just tired."

"You seem pretty blocked," Dottie said, glancing sideways at Alice.

"I was alone," I said.

"You took the pills because you were alone?" said Alice.

"I took the pills because I was alone," I said. "Alone too much." I could see my own face, looking at me. A funny thing. "My father died," I said. "My mother was—" I didn't know how to say it. She didn't like me much, I thought. "I don't know."

"There's nothing like a mother's love," said Frank, reproachfully.

"Thank God," said Janet.

"My mother is my stalwart defender," Dottie said. Her eyes had gotten very round.

"That's lovely," I said. I meant it, too.

"What did you want to say about your mother?" said Alice. Her gaze was very steady. How long had it been my turn?

"She didn't like me much," I said.

"A lot of people think that, things like that," Dottie trilled. "But it's usually a misunderstanding."

"A mother's love is next to God's," said Frank.

"Thank you, Vera," said Alice.

The lights were bright. The circle moved on, the tension around me collapsed. I could feel the cool light from the ceiling panels pouring down over the top of my head. Like cool fingers searching in my hair. I remembered catching my mother crying once. Her face unfamiliar, soft and red. Maybe that was not long after my father died.

Ah, she just couldn't cheer me up, I thought. And there was nothing she hated like failure.

162

The lights were ringing, or buzzing. Alice was trying to reach the buttons on the television to turn down the sound.

She didn't hate you, I thought. She hated to fail.

"We're going to listen to some music," Alice said, and we sat and listened to strings, which were like voices. In my heart I showered Elizabeth Kelly with a deep and stoned compassion.

CHAPTER 11

It was sunrise when I woke again. I was disoriented, and I had to take a panicked inventory of the things I could see from the bed in order to understand where I was and how long I had slept. It was Friday morning. I recovered information bit by bit, picking up flotsam left in the wake of the tranquilizer.

I dozed until breakfast and then ate with Claire in the dining room. She was in a sour mood. I appealed to her expertise. "Claire," I said, "do you ever cheek your meds?"

"I'm taking them," she said. "It's none of your business."

"No, I mean—if I don't want to take mine ... how do you—"

"Oh," she said. "When I was a kid, I did it all the time."

"You were in places like this when you were a kid?"

"I was fifteen the first time, I think. No, fourteen." She peeled the foil from a cup of orange juice.

"How do you do it so they don't notice?"

"You're bold, aren't you?" she said. "Don't be so loud."

"Sorry."

She reached across the table and tore a piece off the cold pancake I was eating, then rolled it between two fingers and dropped it on my tray. "Practice with that," she said. "You have to feel it."

⊕

I practiced with the ball of pancake, and then in our room with a scrap of notebook paper, which I chewed and rolled for so long that it bounced if I dropped it. When med rounds came at twelve thirty, I said nothing, took the cup and water quickly, moved the pills into the side of my mouth, and handed the empty cups back. The nurse looked intently at me, but she left without saying anything. I spat the corroded pills into my hand and put them in my pocket.

Claire, who was coloring in her toenails with a marker, said, "Good job."

I went to sign up for use of the telephone, which I was now allowed to do, since I had been at Mineral Springs for over twenty-four hours. Nick answered on the second ring. "They just called me now to say the transfer hasn't gone through," he said. "I got very irate. I told them I would have an explanation from our account manager at Credit Suisse immediately."

"Oh no."

"I think I'll have some difficulty getting Claude on the phone today. It's the Friday of a holiday weekend."

I laughed. I loved to watch Nick lie. He had an incredible, unsettling fluidity. I always admired his technique, and I was a pretty good liar myself. "Is it?"

"May Day. You know how these Swiss bankers are about May Day. Everybody's off to their chalets."

"I hope you explained all that to them."

"Oh, I did. I gave them a lot of detail about Claude."

"*Pauvre* Claude," I said.

"He'll be in terrible trouble when he gets back to the office on Tuesday," Nick said.

"Nick," I said. "Do you need a kidney or anything? A lung?"

"Keep your organs," he said. "I'll see you soon."

I went to the lounge, where Russell was sitting in a corner, watching the television from a distance of fifteen feet or so. When I came in, he glanced over, shifted in his chair as if about to stand up, and then settled back again instead. I walked to the window and looked out. Another blazing day. I wanted a tentative, cool morning on my own block. I wanted the gauze of new green leaves on the plum tree at the corner. The mornings were usually my own, at home. Max slept late. I liked to sit on the stoop, even on chilly days, drinking tea and looking up and down the street, knowing that Max was upstairs in bed, that the world stopped at my door and my love was at home. The California sunshine showed me a bright slope of baking rocks, the glitter of the springs below. Haze again over the ordinary crowded subdivision at the end of the valley. They might let me out that day for recreation. Hard to say if it would help me, if Max was still in isolation.

Russell said, "Vera, do you have a match?"

I turned. "No, I quit."

There was a muddled intensity to his expression. I remembered that I had told him the day before that I didn't smoke.

I looked at him curiously, and he returned my gaze without blinking. I came over and sat in the chair opposite him.

"Still haven't solved this match problem?" I said.

"They let the new patient out of iso this morning," he said.

I leaned forward. "They did?"

"I saw her in the hallway after breakfast."

"Russell," I said. My mouth was suddenly dry. "Russell. Could you—"

"It looks like they're giving her Thorazine," he interrupted. "Have you seen that? She's got that look."

"What look?"

"It's heavy, that's all. Thorazine is heavy. I hated it."

"Can you talk to her?" I said.

"Do you want to see her?"

"Yes!" I said.

"Are you going to be here?"

"Sure. Yes, sure. I'll stay here all day."

He leaned back. He looked relieved. I had the sense that my presence in his life was deeply stressful. "I'll look around," he said.

He left. I sat in my chair, massaging my knuckles, buzzing discreetly. The cool tones of a soap opera played on the television. Something creaked in the hall.

I wondered why he was helping. I went around it a few times, examined it from the limited angles I had, and decided that he was doing it because there wasn't much else to do, and maybe because he was a good person.

I waited an hour, and then there was a sound at the door and there she was, wearing the same pajamas and bathrobe that I wore, her hair loose and tangled, her steps halting, beginning to cry.

CHAPTER 12

She stopped and put her hand to her mouth. I stood up and the magazine in my lap slid off and cracked spine-first on the floor. Steve turned laboriously around to look at me. Russell was standing behind Max. "This is the lounge!" he said loudly.

I could see what he meant about the Thorazine. She looked shaken and confused, with something unfamiliar in the way she held her face. I was close to tears. I wanted to put my arms around her. I thought I'd better not. I went to her and squeezed her hand, and she fell forward onto my shoulders. I could feel her heart racing in her chest.

"Honey, honey," I said, allowing myself, just for an instant, to put my hand into her hair. I could feel the bored gaze of the others on my back. I set her on her feet.

"How did you get in here?" she whispered.

"You know each other?" someone said.

"Small world," I said over my shoulder.

I led her to the window. Her normal brightness, the quick way she scanned a room, her agility—the way she wove back and forth behind the bar, joining the end of one motion to the beginning of the next, efficient, graceful—were all gone. She had the face of a child. She was bewildered by the difficulty of moving her body. "How did you get in here?" she said again, quietly. I pressed her hand between mine. I wanted to bite it. She had painted her nails a sober pink to see her father and the polish had chipped.

"We'll talk about it later," I said.

"They tricked me," she said. "They put me in a car. I fought them. I don't know who it was. My father went inside and left them."

"You'll never see any of them again," I said.

"My sister," she said.

"Was she there?" I remembered Inez's frantic, tearful exit from the house that morning.

"She tried to stop them. She screamed—" A wobbly smile surfaced. "She screamed bloody murder."

"Inez is okay," I said. "Inez can come for Christmas."

She laughed. Her bathrobe was falling off her shoulders and there was a bruise yellowing on her upper arm. "What is that?" I said.

"I fell, I think." She looked at it, puzzled. "Against the car. The door. The car door."

I permitted myself the pleasure of imagining Il Refugio burning to the ground and her father waving helplessly from an upper window.

"Was St. James there?" I said.

"I don't know. It happened so fast. I went to talk to Aloysius . . . I was angry, I was shouting. I just couldn't believe he would be taken in by people like that. I don't know."

I said, "I thought you had been in an accident."

She was looking out the window. Tears ran down her face. She held my hand. "I called you," she said. "I sneaked it. After seeing the psychiatrist. But they caught me."

"Good girl," I said. The short-haired woman from the day before was watching us from a corner by a potted fig. I leaned close. "I have your car. It's parked just up the hill."

"The Avanti?" she said. "My car."

"We just have to get to it," I whispered. "I have the key. I have a little money too."

"How do we get out?" she said.

"I don't know. Pull the fire alarm? Baby, you have to try not to take those meds." We would have to go in the dark. How would I find her? "Did you see the parking lot on the way in?"

"No."

"It's just there, it's not far. If you go out the main entrance, there's a path that goes to the parking lot, just up the hill. But you'll have to be quick. It's right out in the open. We'll have to find each other quickly in the dark and go."

She looked frightened. "Okay," she said.

"You can do it," I said. When I looked up, the short-haired woman was watching us again. She shifted officiously in her chair and pretended to be interested in the television.

A nurse rapped her knuckles on the doorway. "Maxine," she said. "Time for group. Russell, will we have the pleasure today?"

"I have to write letters," Russell said.

"Maxine? You're hoping for outside privileges, aren't you?"

Max looked at me, pie-eyed. "You should go," I whispered. "Make nice. Be ready tonight."

She hesitated, then brought her open, disoriented face close to mine. "I love you," she said. She breathed the words out and they settled over me. For an instant she was all I could see. Then she was gone.

⊕

There was a single red fire alarm behind a glass panel in the voluntary patients' hallway, and it was directly across from the nurses' station. I walked past it twice, three times, despairing. If I pulled it, they would just wrestle me to the ground and turn it off.

"Miss Kelly, can we help you with something?" said the charge nurse.

"No, no," I said.

I sat reading in my room. Claire was asleep again, whistling through her nose. An orange sunset riled up the place. I kept coming to the conclusion that I would have to set a real fire, rejecting it, coming to it again. I was tired.

Claire tossed and turned and finally took off her eyeshade.

"Claire," I said softly, "what are you in for?"

A nurse passing in the hallway reached around the doorframe and flipped on the lights. Claire looked very sad. "Couldn't get out of bed," she said. "Just ran out of gas."

"Is that all?"

"I was living in a little place I rented. Couldn't get out of bed."

"You can't get out of bed here," I said.

"Can't get out of bed anywhere," she said.

She looked even younger than usual. I heard lights clicking on up and down the hallway, half-hearted cries of irritation. The sun had not yet entirely set, and the electric lights jarred with it. "What about the first time?" I said. "When you were a kid?"

"I practically sawed my arm off with a steak knife. One of those cheapo ones. I went running around the house dripping blood on all the rugs."

"Jesus."

"I can't remember what I was so upset about."

"I'm sure you had your reasons," I said.

"Sure, there were reasons." She turned onto her back and stared at the ceiling. "I want to go to college. My mother says it's too late."

"How old are you?"

"Twenty-two. She says I would just waste their money. That I never finish anything." Her eyes were wet. "What am I supposed to do with all this time?"

"All what time?"

"My life."

I remembered some things about twenty-two—I had felt gossamer-thin, like a strong breeze would disperse me. Like I made only the lightest impression on people and places; like no one would remember me if I were gone. It was hard even to notice my own distress—the mewling of a kitten somewhere deep in the ductwork. How old had I been when I looked around and saw that I had solidified? Twenty-eight? Twenty-nine? Mere minutes ago. I wanted to tell her she would firm up too. I didn't know how to say it. "I was in juvie when I was seventeen," I said instead.

"Yeah? What did you do?"

"I stole my mother's car. I mean, that's how she saw it. I was planning to give it back."

"For how long?"

"I was only gone overnight. The cops came the next morning."

"What, joyriding?"

"Well. No. She was beating the hell out of me and I hit her back. I didn't think I could stick around after that. I drove to my aunt's house in Baltimore."

"Is she sorry now?" said Claire.

"Who, my mother? For calling the cops?"

"Yeah."

This question had never crossed my mind. I marveled at it. "I don't know," I said. "I wouldn't bet on it. But I suppose she's spent a lot of time alone since then."

"My mother wishes I would get married," Claire said. "She wants to get me off her hands."

"Tell her you're a lesbian," I said.

She laughed. "I'd join a convent, but they won't let you lie in bed all day."

"Do you want to be here, Claire?" I said. I leaned a little closer, putting my feet on the floor.

She lay there fiddling with the satin edge of the blanket. "I don't know," she said. "It feels like doing something. When I come out, sometimes I'm happy for a few weeks. Being in here—I go home and it feels like a pretty good time just to wash my hair without asking permission."

"Do you go to group?"

She said darkly, "Do you know, everybody in group was interfered with."

"Everybody?"

"Just about everybody."

"Is it good for you? Group?"

"Sometimes."

"Claire, I'm going to ask you to do something," I said. "And you can say yes or no. I really won't think any less of you if you say no. But I have to ask you. And if you say no, then I won't do my part of it either, just don't tell anyone I asked."

"Oh, Christ," she said.

I sat there bugging my eyes out at her, wishing I had the time for something more subtle.

"I don't want any part of any drugs," she said. "I don't do that stuff."

"It's not about drugs."

She relaxed. "What, then?"

⊕

At 8:15 PM I went into one of the empty rooms in the voluntary corridor with an issue of *Redbook* and a box of matches borrowed from Claire. I shut the door behind me and kept the lights off. My hands were shaking. This could be very, very stupid, I thought. Very stupid. But Claire would come right away. A minute only, two minutes. Didn't the girls used to set fires at the Barrington School all the time? Did anybody ever get so much as singed?

I piled the slick pages in the wastepaper basket and dropped in a match. With a faint *whoosh*, a perfume ad went up, the creeping flame burning blue in the dark room, like the gas jet on a stove top. Blue, then green, as it worked its way across a field of daisies in a laundry detergent spread. I hovered there for an instant, surprised that the ink in the pages changed the color of the fire. Then I stripped a pillowcase off the bed and fed it in. I dragged the wastepaper basket to the center of the room and then slipped out, leaving the door open a crack.

A nurse in the hall glanced at me as I passed. I didn't hold her eye. It was so sloppy, so obvious. But I needed only these few seconds. Maybe it was for the best if they knew it was me in the end, anyway—it would keep anybody else from getting in trouble, and I would be gone. How could they touch me, really, once I was beyond these walls? I passed Claire, heading in the other direction, just as she was supposed to. Her slippers flapped against the floor in her usual way—she always walked like she was in stacked heels. Her face was completely ordinary, a mask of boredom and melancholy. I was impressed with her. She was keeping her head. I felt that I was throwing off sparks, drawing the attention of everyone I passed. I reached the end of the row of patients' rooms and turned the corner toward the reception area and the front doors. Behind me, I heard Claire shout, "There's a fire! Jesus, somebody come help me!" A babble of other voices rose up, and then the fire alarm began to shriek.

Lights flashed high up on the walls. A custodian who had been walking toward me picked up his pace. A woman sitting in one of the administrative offices looked uncertainly around. "It's not a drill," I said to her. "There's smoke in the patients' hall."

The receptionist at the front had come out from behind the check-in desk and was standing in the entrance hall, looking like she had been expecting me. "I'm one of the fire marshals for this wing," she said, pointing out the front doors. "Head right out there and wait."

"Oh, thank you," I said.

I pushed through the doors and out into the dark. Behind me, footsteps approached as the bulk of the patients were ushered along the evacuation route. I bolted. The doors behind me were opening, and an irritated voice said, "Quickly please, quickly, you're being timed." I tucked my useless slippers under my arm and ducked away from the pavement and its single mounted lamp, down the brush-covered slope. I would have to cut across the scarp and climb up to the parking lot hand over hand. I didn't know if I was strong enough. I was below the hospital now, out of sight. My eyes were adjusting. It was a clear night with a good moon, and once I was away from the lights of the building I could see well enough, although distances were hard to judge, and I had to clutch at bushes and feel for purchase on the steep ground with my bare feet. Pebbles and dirt showered down the slope away from me. I inched toward the dusty terrace where the parking lot was, gripping the sage as I went. I couldn't see the group of patients, but I could hear the nurses beginning to count heads. Faint traffic noise drifted up from a road in the valley. I stepped on something sharp and crumpled; I had to crouch and breathe through my nose for a few seconds to recover myself.

Above me, in front of the hospital, people continued to assemble, their voices raised in annoyance. I didn't know if the involuntary patients mustered with the voluntaries or if they might be on the other side of the building. I had to hope that Max knew where the main entrance was, that she could find her way around to the parking lot on her own, that she had a clear enough head. I could see the cars gleaming in the dark ahead and above me, and I moved faster, straightening up for a few paces where the ground was soft and I could dig my toes into the face of the slope. I was drenched in sweat and I suspected that my foot was bleeding. I had dropped the slippers somewhere behind me. No matter, they wouldn't have been much help to me anyway. The ground leveled out for fifty feet or so, and I darted across. I was just below the parking lot. I could see the group of patients and staff in front of the hospital, a collection of crossed arms. The night was turning cold. They were backlit, and I couldn't pick out their faces. I had a sudden vision of myself as one of the tiny figures clinging to the face of Mount Rushmore at the end of *North by Northwest*. I pulled myself up the rocky surface, arm over arm. A clod of earth gave way and I slid backward, battering my elbows as I did so. In a frantic push, I regained the ground I had lost. Warmth was turning to pain across my shoulders and back. My wet hair clung to my face and neck.

A guardrail marked the lip of the lot, and with a last heave I caught hold of a stanchion. I crawled under the steel cable and sat panting on the dirt. The Avanti was parked a few yards away, pale in the moonlight. I tried to get up but found that my body wouldn't respond. It would take a few minutes. My arms and legs were shaking.

Where was she? I pivoted and stared into the dark. The figures in front of the hospital were going back inside. The rocky slope below was empty. The pathway was empty as well, its lone light shining down. I examined my feet: the first and second toes of my right foot were dark with blood. My over-laundered institutional pajamas were streaked with dirt, torn at one knee. Where was she?

I could stand now. I checked my bra—the key, my license, and the little bit of money were still there. I got up carefully, as if managing the strings of a marionette. My knees held. I got the door of the Avanti open and settled my filthy body into it.

I hesitated over the question of turning the key in the ignition. The last stragglers were going inside now. I would delay a few minutes. It was strange to be sitting there: everything in the car was just as I had left it. It had only been a day and a half.

About five minutes passed. It was hard to know. I had no watch, of course. The portico in front of the hospital was empty. I drummed on my lips with my fingers. I tried not to entertain the thought that she might not come. What would I do then? I couldn't go back. I would have to free her somehow from the outside, which would be impossible. I tried counting my breaths. Fifty breaths, and she had not come. One hundred breaths, one hundred fifty. I changed from counting breaths to singing a college fight song that Peach had taught me over the course of a very long night once, years ago—verses that went on and on. When I had finished it, I started again. Where was Peach tonight? There wasn't enough air in the car, somehow. I rolled down the window. The night was so clear, the mountain such an overwhelming presence.

A dark figure came around the far end of the hospital, uphill from the pathway. Two figures. One large, one small. Dressed in pajamas. I sat up and put my hands on the wheel, straining my eyes. They picked their way across the slope. They were in full view of the front of the hospital. I turned the key in the ignition and put my bare feet on the pedals. The engine seemed catastrophically loud. It was her—I saw the flutter of her hands as she slipped and steadied herself. I pounded the wheel. The other one—they were close now, they had a much easier route than I had—I started to laugh. It was Russell, following along like a friendly bear.

I jumped out of the car as they approached, and they hurried toward me. Max was beaming, unsteady on her feet. I wrapped my arms around her, feeling all my bruises as I did so, breathing in the sharp scent of her unwashed hair, her warm sweat, the floral traces of her crème rinse. "Get in, get in," I said.

"You're all dirty," she said. "Are you bleeding?"

"Russell, are you coming? Get in," I said.

He got into the back seat, turning his knees sideways to fit. I helped Max into the front. Her hair kept swinging in front of her face, and she had a hard time folding herself in, understanding where her arms and legs should be. The hospital glowed silently at the end of the walkway. The moon was like a floodlight at a high school football game. I dropped into my own seat, put the car in gear, and made a hard loop out of the parking lot and onto the road. I was overwhelmed with gratitude for the car and its ambitious, ready engine, which ate up the steep incline with no apparent difficulty and eased happily into third gear as we crested it.

"Are you okay, baby?" I said to Max.

She was crying. She put her hand on my arm. "They used to say it when we were kids," she said. "'We'll send you to the hospital. You belong in the hospital.' And I didn't have you then."

"Did you know I was coming?" I said.

"I hoped you were," she said. "I thought you were. I had to think you were. But it felt—it felt like I had disappeared."

"Of course I was coming," I said.

From the back seat Russell said, "I'm so sorry, but I have to vomit."

"Oh!" I pulled over. There were no lights around. Russell climbed out of the car, took two steps, and threw up into a bush. He came quickly back to the car, wiping his mouth.

"I'm so sorry," he said again. "Nervous stomach."

"Max, your purse is back there," I said. "Russell, maybe there's a Kleenex."

He rummaged. Max said, "I love you." Then she let go of my arm and switched the radio on. We drove under a fat moon. I was so happy. We were free.

"I thought, at first," I said. "I thought all kinds of horrible things."

"I knew you would come," she said.

"I know sometimes I—" Some things had been obvious in my mind these past days, as I found my way here, but it was difficult to find words for them. "I know sometimes I—don't talk enough or I—I'm not clear—"

"You're clear enough," she said.

"I don't know what I would do if something happened to you," I said.

"I know," she said.

"I never want to be apart," I said.

"We'll never be apart," she said.

CHAPTER 13

At a gas station I said, "How much money do we have, between the three of us?"

Max said, "I don't have anything. I had some money in my pocket when I left, but that's all in the hospital."

Russell was embarrassed. "I don't have anything either," he said. "All my things are in the lockers."

"Right," I said. "Right." I looked down at myself, and then at them, in their cleaner and more intact pajamas. The cut on my foot stung from working the pedals. The three of us looked like what we were. We looked like we had liberated ourselves from a mental institution. We were parked under a Sunoco sign along the highway. I reached into my bra and pulled out my bundle of bills. "I have twenty-seven dollars."

"Okay," said Max. "Okay. Well, we just need a motel room."

"We can get a motel room for tonight," I said. "But we need clothes and food too. Or I do. I need shoes. We have to get to LAX by four tomorrow." I swiveled toward the back seat. "Where to, Russell?"

He was surprised by the question. In fact he had a generally surprised, remote quality, like a cloistered monk suddenly forced into society. He sat up straight in the limited space he had and said, "Home, if I could."

"Where is home?"

"Los Angeles."

"That's convenient. You don't happen to live by the airport, do you?"

"No," he said. "Well, not that far."

I searched his face. Some things were occurring to me. "Why were you in there?" I said. "In the hospital?"

"I'd been staying up all night," he said. "Spending money I shouldn't. Long phone calls."

"They locked you up for phone calls?"

"I was manic," he said. "But I don't want to be in that hospital anymore."

"Are you going to be all right at home?"

"My sister comes and checks on me."

"She'll be surprised to see you."

"She might be."

How long would it take them to notice we had gone? Max was an object of special attention. She had no doubt come with her own instructions. I was uneasy. The car was so conspicuous. We were so conspicuous.

Filling the tank ate into our money. We stopped at a burger stand and then pulled right back out on the road, the car redolent of fry grease. Half an hour of driving yielded only a Holiday Inn, which would have taken most of the money we had left. I didn't see how we would find a place to sleep and have enough

184

left over to get through the following day. My lack of shoes pressed on me. I might be able to find something to wear among Max's things, but I was bigger than she was and we did not wear the same size shoe. The banks were closed.

"Russell," I said. The solution now seemed obvious, so obvious that I wondered why he hadn't thought of it first. "Can we stay at your place tonight?" I glanced in the rearview mirror.

"It's a mess," he said finally.

"*Russell*," Max said, and it was the voice I had heard her use a thousand times when a friend was being stubborn, resisting some idea she had, refusing to have more fun, go to another bar, dance another song, have another slice of cake, and I thought, There she is, she's come back. "Russell, we don't care if it's a mess."

"Of course you're welcome," he said hastily. "It's just—not in a condition for guests."

"Russell."

"Let's go," he said. "It's all right."

"Good man," said Max.

"I live in Culver City," he said.

"Can you direct me?" I said.

"Sure."

⊕

We took Russell's exit around eleven o'clock. The food had fortified me, but the fatigue of dragging myself across a hundred yards of rocks was catching up by then, and I drove through a blur of orange and soft gray. How can it be, I thought groggily, that there is so much here? So many streets, so many boxy little houses, so many neighborhoods and exits and developments, repeating and repeating, world without end. The bricky distinctness of Brooklyn was strange to recall. Palm trees stood black against the glow of the sky, gangly and out of scale. Each house was abutted by its neat garage. Russell said, "It's not much."

"Culver City? I always liked it over here," Max said quickly. "In high school I would drive around here, go to the movies."

"Where are you from?" Russell said.

I sensed Max's embarrassment from the passenger seat. "We live in New York," I said.

Max said, "I grew up here, in Los Angeles."

"Where?"

"Bel Air," she said, all in.

"Oh!" he said. "Beautiful."

"It sours on you," she said.

Russell leaned forward between the seats. "Turn right there," he said. "It's the fourth on the left."

I made the turn and pulled into Russell's driveway. It was a flat-roofed ranch house, like all the others on its block, with a short space of bare yard in front. "Can we park in the garage?" I said, nervous about the car.

"All right," he said. "Let me get it open."

"Thank you." I took the key out of the ignition. Quiet descended, with a distant hum of freeways. Russell climbed out of the car, but then he stopped, standing in the driveway, looking at the house.

"I don't have my keys," he said.

"Of course," I said. "Right."

"My sister has a key."

Max and I glanced at each other. Hard to say how much discretion the unknown sister would have on encountering the three of us in the condition we were in, driving this car.

"I think I can get in through the back," he said.

We watched him walk around the garage to the back of the house. A car rumbled down the street behind us, and we both stopped breathing until it had passed.

"Four o'clock tomorrow," Max said.

"Counting the minutes," I said.

The garage door lurched and then lifted. Russell appeared beneath it, triumphant. I nosed the car in. In the headlights I could see a terrific pile of buckets and hoses and crates and paint cans and lamps—a weird profusion of unshaded lamps. We got out and Russell led us in through a side door into the house. With an apologetic chuckle, he hit the lights.

I stepped back reflexively. Max and I goggled at each other. We were in a small kitchen, and the counters were piled in slopes to the bottoms of the cabinets with papers, dishes, plastic containers, and disassembled appliances—more lamps, toasters, clocks, stereo equipment, and unidentifiable parts. A pathway of bare floor led from where we stood through another door into the next room, but the rest of the linoleum was occupied with what appeared to be a disemboweled lawn mower, more papers, more appliances, and more dishes.

"The sofa folds out," Russell said. He picked his way past us, humming. We followed. In the living room, where books and newspapers and more components of more machines were thick on the floor, on the end tables, and on a set of industrial-style shelving opposite the shaded windows, he valiantly cleared off a rust-colored love seat. We watched him kick a coil of wire and what appeared to be a muffler out of the way in order to fold it out. It settled with a creak and a twang of old springs.

"I'm sorry," he said. "I know it's—"

"It's perfect," I said.

The thought of him searching through the house for sheets was mortifying. Max and I assured him that we were so exhausted we wanted to lie down right away, that we would be asleep before our heads touched the cushions, and he pointed out the bathroom—a well-worn path beaten to its door—and withdrew.

Max whispered, "Do you think there are mice?"

"I have no doubt," I said. "But to be fair, there are mice in our house too."

We turned out the lights and lay on the twin mattress. It smelled like dust. We clutched each other; we fit together so easily. At the touch of her hair against my face, I started to cry. She stroked my back. I had been so afraid.

CHAPTER 14

I woke feeling better than I had in years, despite how badly I needed a bath, despite my returning hunger and the difficulties of the day that lay ahead. Waking in an unfamiliar place was like being twenty again, but not alone this time, not confused. Max stretched and pointed her toes. "Jesus, I ache," she said. "I forgot what it's like to sleep on a twin."

"It must be early," I said. Molten sun lined the closed shades. I clambered to the windows and raised them. The light was powerful, overwhelming, as if the sun were rising across the street. The sky was burnished and immense. There was simply nothing in the way.

"Max, let's come back to LA sometime and spend a lot of money and just lie by a pool all day," I said.

"Let's never come here again," Max said.

We dared not attempt to salvage food or coffee from the kitchen. Even opening the cabinets seemed risky. We shuffled around the small parts of the living room that were passable, trying to be quiet, hoping we would fail and Russell would wake up. A clock in the kitchen indicated that it was just after six o'clock in the morning. Max found a paperback of *Valley of the Dolls* and read for a while. I searched her suitcase and found a blouse I could wear, but the jeans she had packed wouldn't button and the skirts wouldn't zip. I had several inches and ten or fifteen pounds on her. I twirled in the peasant blouse and hospital pajamas.

"*Très chic*," said Max. "We'll buy you something. To go with your new shoes."

When Russell did appear, he had washed and shaved and was wearing street clothes, and he seemed invigorated, happier.

"Have you spoken to your sister?" I said. "Did the hospital call her when you left? Or did they call the police?"

"They called her. They always call her first. I don't think they like to get the police involved. Their reputation, you know. I spoke to her last night. She's coming by this afternoon with a copy of my key."

"So they must have called my father," Max said. "We need to get out of here."

"Yes. We need to buy shoes and things. We should go while it's still early," I said. "Anyway, I'm hungry. Russell, I'm so sorry, but do you have anything at all I could put on my feet? I can't get them into Max's shoes."

He withdrew and came back with a pair of cracked huaraches that extended two generous inches past the tips of my toes. I had to shuffle to keep them on.

"Do you need directions?" Russell said.

"Aren't you coming with us?" Max said.

"Oh, there's no need," Russell said. "You have things to do."

"Russell, don't be ridiculous."

"Are you hungry?" I said.

"I have things here," he said, unpersuasively, pointing toward the kitchen.

"Please let us get you breakfast," I said. "Where would we be without you?"

⊕

We went out to the car and drove the early morning streets of Culver City. In light traffic, in these residential neighborhoods, the car was as subtle as a ticker tape parade. A man out watering his roses turned 180 degrees, hands on his hips, to watch us pass by. Max was oblivious to this. She was driving now, the drugs having faded from her system, and her pleasure at being behind the wheel of her old car again muted any other impressions. "What are we going to do with it?" she said, a little sadly, at a stoplight between a supermarket and an outpost of the California Department of Motor Vehicles.

"We'll have to leave it," I said.

"At the airport?"

"That's what I was thinking."

"It's a shame. Can't we give it to Russell?"

Russell, sitting in the back seat, looked alarmed. This idea felt beautiful for a moment—but no.

"He'd get in trouble," I said. "The papers are in your mother's name, not yours."

She looked at me, shocked. "They changed the registration?"

"They must have." I touched the glove box. "I checked it."

A new tension entered her arms and shoulders. She looked around. "Well," she said. "Well, at least it's not my father's."

We stopped at another drive-through for breakfast and parked this time to eat, rustling paper wrappers and cardboard boxes. I kept touching Max's leg, her shoulder. Russell hummed in the back seat, drinking coffee. I walked to a pay phone at the edge of the lot and called Nick. He picked up, even though it was before dawn in New York. I apologized for waking him and told him we would fly home that afternoon. He cheered, his voice rough from sleep.

"We'll see you soon," I said. "We'll make you a brisket."

"You'd better," he said.

I walked back across the asphalt toward the car. I loved to see Max from a distance like this: focused, silent, looking out at traffic passing by, the whole scene a scrap of a life that might be someone else's, but was mine.

I got back in the passenger seat, and Max crumpled up the remains of her breakfast and turned the key in the ignition. "Where to, Russell?" she said.

"Back home, thank you," he said.

We drove the quiet streets back to the house. In the drive-way we sat for a moment, and Max said again, "Thank you for your help."

"Well, thank you for the lift," Russell said.

"Give us your telephone number," I said, "and your address. We'll send cards."

We found a paper and pencil in the glove box, and he wrote it all down. We got out and hugged him, which he accepted with more energy than I had expected. It was an enveloping hug, and then he turned and went up the two steps to his unlocked front door. "Bon voyage," he called, and went inside.

We were alone. The atmosphere in the car shifted. We clung together for a minute, and then Max, with renewed energy, turned on the radio and reversed out of the driveway. I was reminded in a funny way of late nights when I was sixteen, seventeen, before I was sent away, driving with friends through the streets of Chevy Chase, circling the blue and red lights of ice cream stands out in Montgomery County, feeling that we were invisible to adults and a beacon to other teenagers, that we looked cool, that we were cool, and that no one could tell us what to do.

Max drove until we spotted a Sears nested beside a freeway on-ramp. We sat in the parking lot, preparing to go in. Max produced a compact from her bag, and we looked ourselves over and then wished we hadn't. My hair had fanned out and was losing its curl, and I smelled sharply of sweat.

"If somebody asks, we'll tell them we're locked out of our house," I said. "We stepped out to get the paper and got locked out."

"Both of us?"

"Sure, both of us."

"Three-quarters dressed?" Max was outfitted like a normal person.

"Yes."

"And after that, did we fight a bear?"

"Maybe we did." I tried to scrape the remaining dried blood off the cuticles of my toes, and then put them gingerly back into the enormous huaraches. I should have cleaned up more at Russell's, but the bathroom had been mysteriously crowded with foam rubber padding. A woman in an immaculate skirt suit walked past the car, her pocketbook swinging, her hair freshly waved. I sighed. "Here we go," I said.

The sliding doors of Sears admitted us to a chilly hush. It was still quite early, not yet nine thirty. Mannequins stood on plinths. The place had an atmosphere of readiness, braced for the hordes who would come on their lunch breaks or in the long afternoon, towing children. It was comforting and familiar as we walked around—the dangling price tags, the racks of discount perfumes, the bins of ladies' underwear. Max stopped at a table piled with folded blue jeans. "This is your size, isn't it?"

"Sure," I said, hesitating.

"You never wear blue jeans," Max said.

"Now's not the time for vanity," I said.

"On the run in dungarees," Max said. "What dire straits."

I let her drape the jeans over my shoulder. Far away across the floor, I saw a saleswoman stop in her rounds to look at us, adjusting large glasses.

"Shoes," I said. "I need shoes."

The shoe department was miles away. We traversed the outer reaches of the store. In the distance, the saleswoman appeared and reappeared, watching us, like the sea lions in the surf that follow people walking down the beach.

"There are eyes on us," I said.

"It's all right," Max said, squeezing my hand. "What can she say? We're not stealing anything."

I checked the price on the jeans and subtracted it from what we had. "We don't have much left for shoes," I said. "Maybe we should get something cheaper."

"It'll take too long to find something. Those are on sale already."

We passed lingerie and turned into the shoe department. "The instant I get home I'm going to throw this bra away," I said, tugging at the one I was wearing, shifting my arms. "I've been wearing it too long. My relationship with it is ruined."

"Let's get you some brogues," Max said. "Some big butch brogues."

"Let's go to men's and get a coverall to go with them." I took a pair of sandals off a rack, checked the size. The saleswoman was approaching. "Max, she's coming."

"Don't act so suspicious," Max said. "It's not a crime to look a mess."

"It feels like it is."

The saleswoman arrived. "Ladies, do you need any assistance?" she said.

"We're all right, thank you," Max said.

"We're just going to buy these shoes," I said, holding up the sandals.

"We got locked out," Max said.

"Yes," I said, relieved at the prompt. "We went out to get the paper and got locked out. We weren't dressed."

She looked doubtfully from me to Max and back again. "I'll just walk you to the register," she said finally.

"Oh!" Max said, her eyes going round. "That's not necessary!"

"It's no trouble," she said.

"All right," Max said. "We'll just buy these things and be right out of your hair."

Like the Israelites crossing the desert, we walked from the shoe department to the cash registers in front, trailed by the saleswoman. I could feel her eyes on my back. In my mind I counted and recounted the money we had against the things we were buying. I couldn't be sure of the price tag on the shoes. I thought it had said $3.99, but I wasn't certain. If it was $3.99, then we would be all right, with $0.43 left over. We could eat on the flight. We could get back to New York with $.43. I wished we had had more time to make our selections. The saleswoman's slacks swished behind us.

When we arrived at the checkout lines, the saleswoman stepped behind an empty register herself and waved us forward. I saw now that her name tag said SHEILA—FLOOR MGR. At the next checkout line, a teenage clerk watched us with interest.

Max, smiling, put our things on the belt. I watched Sheila key in the numbers. The shoes that Max had picked up were not $3.99. They were $4.99.

"Oh," I said, my heart falling. "We just—"

"Your total is $14.57," said Sheila.

"We just have to substitute a different pair of shoes," I said.

"How much do we have?" Max said.

"Fourteen dollars," I whispered.

The teenage clerk had turned all the way around at her own post and was chewing gum.

"I'll just go back and get something else," Max said, reaching for the shoes. She looked, all at once, exhausted. The chirp in her voice was gone. Sheila stopped her. She reached across the belt and lifted the price tag to look at it.

"Well," she said. She cleared her throat. "This is a misprint."

"It is?" Max said.

"I just sold a pair of these shoes yesterday," said Sheila. "They were $3.99."

"Oh, wow," Max said. "Oh, wow."

"That's terrific," I said. "Thank you."

"It's a misprint," Sheila said again. She wouldn't look at us. I gave her all our money and she counted out forty-three cents in change.

"Thank you," I said again, and we walked back out into the sunshine, carrying the bag.

I changed in the car, shrugging and shimmying into the jeans, and then dug around for some pins for my hair. Max offered me a lipstick from the bottom of her purse. She looked sweet and demure in the dress she had packed. "God, you look terrific," I said.

She laughed and kissed me. I said, without planning it, "I read your libretto."

Her face went blank.

"No, no," I said. "Don't be angry with me, please. I didn't know where you were. It was like talking to you. And I wouldn't have found the hospital without it. It's unlisted—so it wasn't until I read what you wrote—Nick called the foundation and got the address."

She crossed her arms and looked out through the windshield.

"I'm sorry," I said. "I was desperate to talk to you."

"That's how you found the hospital?" she said.

"Yes."

"It's private," she said.

"I know."

She looked at me. "Did you like it?"

"I could see it all," I said, relieved. "I thought it was wonderful."

"You can't read music," she said.

"I can read words all right," I said.

She put the key in the ignition and pulled her seat belt on. "Maybe I should have let you read it, anyway. In the first place."

"It's all right to have private things."

"I was just afraid it was all stupid," she said.

"Stupid?"

"Making up all these things. This monomania. Inventing conversations."

"Someday I'm going to buy you a piano," I said.

"Don't be so dashing," she said. "I can't stand it."

We drove aimlessly. I felt that we were on the verge of something. Max hummed to herself. I thought of our house, our bed. When this would all be over and we could be alone. We would have to call Nick from the airport, beg his indulgence one more time for a ride. Our tally with him was endless.

"I wonder about your mother," I said.

"Me too," Max said.

"Does she know about St. James?" I said.

"Inez has probably told her by now," Max said. A commercial came on the radio, and she changed the station. "I've never seen her fight for anything. I don't know if she'll fight for her money. I don't know if she knows how."

"She must have lawyers," I said.

"That kind of money," Max said. "People don't know how to handle it. You know what? I hope for St. James's sake he never gets his hands on it. From the most compassionate part of my soul. It would vaporize him. A person like that."

"A person like that?"

"He wants it too badly."

"Did it vaporize your grandfather?" I said. The question was impolite, but something about this bothered me, the idea that wanting money was for people who had none, that those who had it had ended up that way accidentally, on their way to somewhere else. But probably she was not saying that at all.

She glanced at me. "Maybe it did. He never spoke to his family. His brothers and sisters. His parents died when he was young. But it's hard to know. I only ever knew him rich." She turned the car onto a boulevard where magenta flowers grew along the median. "It did something to him. That's why I was so interested in Sister Aimee. He acted like he owed her something. I wondered if he was worried about his soul."

"Worried about the eye of that needle," I said.

"Could be."

"What about the other way?" I said.

"What other way?"

"What does it do to a person to lose money like that?" I said. She looked sharply at me. "A person. You mean me?"

"Yeah."

She thought about it. I realized there was a part of me that wanted her to acknowledge the gap between us, as she had failed to do when we were together in Il Refugio. It was silly and ungenerous; what needed to be said? Only that she had grown up on Olympus and I hadn't, that practically nobody else in the world had, and that for all she had suffered, there had been a time when she had lived like a child god. That there were worse ways to suffer, maybe. But why rank them against each other? And what could I know about it?

"When they cut me off, I had never handled a check," she said. "I didn't understand anything about money. I had hardly touched money until I went to Vassar, and then I only knew how to do one thing—go to the bank in Poughkeepsie and give my name to the teller. They would send a man out and we would go to his office and he would count out the money for the month for me. And then after everything happened, I had nothing—I mean I didn't have a dollar, Vera, I lived off my girl-friend for a couple of days and then she got me a job and they paid me cash. I was probably twenty-four before I ever cashed a check, and I had to ask an old woman in the line at the bank how to do it. When they cut me off, I didn't know how to book a train ticket or fry an egg. One of my shoelaces broke, and I sat down and cried. I didn't have any idea where a person goes to buy a shoelace."

We passed a police cruiser double-parked at the curb, a cop leaning against the hood to eat a sandwich in paper. I watched him look at us, and then look again. My lungs filled and stopped. I said nothing. In the rearview I saw him straighten up and walk around to the driver's side of the car.

"I don't know how you raise a kid like that," Max said. "I was so helpless. And I didn't even know it. Inez is still helpless like that, for all I know. I thought I was sophisticated, worldly. I didn't know a goddamn thing. They taught my brother the business, they taught him everything. They left me and Inez upstairs with the dancing teachers."

The cop car pulled away from the curb and into traffic, and the siren started up. Max glanced in the mirror. "No," she said.

"That's for us," I said.

"Oh no," she said.

The cop was a block behind, with heavy traffic in between.

"They must have reported it stolen," she said.

"Maybe not," I said. "Maybe it's a coincidence."

"But they're going to ask for the registration."

I felt very light and empty. Panic scrubbed me out. I had run from police before but not like this. Not in broad daylight, in an American city, with my only identification giving my real name and address, and not with my girlfriend, who was nervy and improvisational but fundamentally a civilian.

"Should I pull over?" Max said, her voice tight. "I don't want to go to jail, Vera."

"We have space," I said. "A whole block."

"You think?" she said, looking in the mirror, and I saw her take in this new thing. The idea of doing this. She reached over and switched off the radio.

"We don't have to," I said. "We can take our chances with them."

We were approaching a yellow light. As I said this, it turned red, and Max pressed the accelerator.

"Easy," I said.

We sailed through. She shifted into third. The engine hiccupped and then dug in and surged forward.

"Easy," I said again. "We don't want to look like we're running yet."

She eased off the gas and turned right at the next light, cutting off a more timid driver in the lane beside us. I watched an irritated face spin away. We were on a broad, sleepy avenue now, the midmorning sun picking up the gleam of parked cars and the silicate glitter of the pavement. She restrained herself, keeping just above the speed limit. She ducked around a bread truck in the left lane and then hurried past a city bus lumbering to a stop on the right. I noticed that I was gripping the dashboard. I tugged on my seat belt and looked over at hers. It was on. She caught a green light and went straight through. Behind us, I saw the ponderous grille of the police cruiser make the same turn we had.

"He's still there," I said.

She was chewing her lip. She looked like a doll in her dress. Her knees were bare, her heels braced against the floor.

"Do you know this neighborhood?" I said.

"It's been a long time," she said. She took a left, down a narrow one-way, between the featureless flanks of a grocery store on one side and a hardware store on the other. We passed two blocks of low apartment complexes and small parking lots. The cop was still behind us. "Well, I guess it's clear we're running now," I said. In the rearview I could see him on his radio. "I don't know, I don't know." It would have been different if I were driving. From the passenger seat, I felt a compulsion to help, but I didn't know the streets here. An overpass appeared before us, traffic buzzing over it, and Max drove into the shadows underneath and turned right to follow it. At a break, where another street cut diagonally through its immense columns, she turned abruptly and to my shock began to drive straight down the concrete service path in the middle, which was not a road at all. A couple of loaders and graders were parked there, and she spun the wheel wide to loop around them and then regained the center of the path, shifted into fourth, and pushed the gas pedal to the floor. I was pressed back against my seat. The engine exulted.

"Ohhhh oh oh," I said. I covered my eyes.

"Is he still back there?"

I turned in my seat. "I don't see him." It was hard to be sure. The sun was bright and the shadows were deep under the overpass, and the columns interposed themselves.

"Where should we ditch it?" Max said.

"The car? Are we ditching it?"

"We knew we couldn't take it with us anyway," she said. "You still don't see him?"

"No, I don't think so," I said. Max swerved around a pile of concrete blocks. I covered my eyes. Traffic streamed by, unawares, along the surface streets on either side. I thought I saw a police car on the far side of the overpass, but when I looked again it was only an ordinary sedan.

"So you think we should leave it here?" Max said. "Under here?"

"Wouldn't it be better to leave it somewhere it can blend in with other cars?" I said.

The car sluiced straight through an enormous puddle. Sheets of water went up like fins.

"I thought maybe we better quit while we're ahead," she said. "I'm sure they got the license plate."

"All right," I said.

She slowed and then rolled to a stop behind one of the monumental columns. She was out of breath. It took her a moment to relax her grip on the wheel and lean back. Then she seemed to remember that we were in a hurry, and she flung her seat belt off and tumbled out of the car, dragging her purse after her. I got out too and we stood facing each other over the roof, both of us wide-eyed and panting. A man standing in front of a gas station out in the sunlight looked at us impassively, drinking from a paper cup. The place where we stood was airy and dim and all out of proportion with us, like a cathedral.

"Do you have everything?" Max said, hauling out her suitcase.

"Yes," I said. "I mean, I don't have anything, but I have all of it."

"Come," she said, then stopped. "God, there's nobody on the street."

"You were expecting New York," I said.

"I was expecting New York."

We walked out past the gas station, smoothing our clothes. The man turned to watch us pass. Max looked back once at her car. Sirens whooped in the distance. We rounded the corner of a garage advertising California emissions inspections. The siren sounded again, closer this time. Max started and went into a jog, and I caught her hand to slow her down. "We're just walking," I said. "They're blocks away. Here, look." At the next corner, a discount department store had its excess inventory out on the sidewalk on tables—piles of children's sandals and tin cookware, a heap of sunglasses tangled together like crabs in a fish market. I pulled her into the store. Large windows, partly covered with poster board advertising sales, looked out on the street.

"I'll just," she murmured, putting her hands into a circular rack of girls' Easter dresses on clearance, doing a half-hearted pantomime of shopping. I navigated past a towering cage filled with beach balls and looked out. The sirens were much closer now, and as I watched, two police cars rounded the far corner, cruised past the store, and disappeared down the next block. I turned back to look at Max, who stood in the froth of little dresses. The place was cavernous. Besides two women in head scarves shopping nearby, I saw no one. A persistent ding in the distance suggested an unseen cashier.

"Maybe we should change clothes again," Max said.

"We have forty-three cents," I said.

"Right, right," she said.

I went over to her and briefly set my forehead on her shoulder. "How in the hell do we get to the airport?" I said.

"The bus?" she said.

"The bus," I breathed. "How much is the fare?"

"Well, I hope to God it's not twenty-five cents."

I had a vision of the two of us panhandling for seven cents in front of the garage on the corner.

"Do you know," she said, "I don't think I've ever been on an LA bus."

"Is it rude to say I'm not surprised?" I said.

"A little. How long should we stay in here?"

"Until my heart slows down." The store, with its buzzing fluorescent lights and worn tile, felt like the safest place in Los Angeles. "I'll ask the cashier where we can get a bus to LAX."

"Okay. Try not to look like a fugitive," she said.

"You've been pretty cool all day," I said. "You'd think you were the professional."

The cashier was a teenager in an ill-fitting uniform jacket that buttoned down the side, like something from *The Jetsons*. She was leaning on the counter, but she straightened up when I approached and swept her hair back.

"Is there a bus nearby," I said, "that goes to the airport?"

She looked blank, and then pity and confusion went to war on her face. "From *here*?" she said. "That's *two* buses."

"Is the transfer free?" I said.

"It's two buses and you have to walk," she said. "Yeah, the transfer is free. You just keep your slip." She took a transit map out from under the counter and unfolded it. It was ancient, the fold lines a white grid of missing ink. "You get on here, and you transfer there. It'll take you a while."

"How much is the bus?"

"It's a quarter."

As she said this, my eye fell on the penny dish beside the register. She and I looked levelly at each other over it.

"I need seven cents," I said.

"That's not what it's for," she said, without conviction.

"It's very important," I said.

She shifted and glanced around the empty store. "They're not my pennies," she said.

"God bless you," I said, a sentiment that I had never before found anywhere in my heart. I counted out seven pennies and walked away.

⊕

So it was that we returned to LAX five days after we had landed there, with zero dollars and zero cents in our pockets, our feet battered, our hair full of dust. We descended from the bus only forty-five minutes before our flight was scheduled to depart. The terminal was busy, clean, strafed by birds. We called Nick collect from a pay phone and told him when we would land.

"They called me this morning," he said. "They said you checked out against medical advice."

"You could say I did that."

"And they asked about the check again. They'll be waiting a while."

Troops of beautiful young women lounged precisely with their luggage. Glossy men stood at coffee counters, reading magazines. No one took any notice of us at all. We felt invisible, the most comfortable state possible. We hovered near our gate, famished, and rushed on when we were called, almost giddy with relief and anticipation of the in-flight meal. In our seats we held hands, our knuckles white. Max turned to the window, lifted the shade, and brushed tears from her lashes.

"Never again," she said.

I thought of the car under the overpass, my shoes and suitcase and bag in a locker somewhere in the staff rooms at Mineral Springs. The unfolding grift at Il Refugio. I had always found it easy to leave things behind. Unfinished business had little hold over me. I wasn't sure Max was the same.

"Never," I said.

We flew east, an accelerated sunset at our backs.

CHAPTER 15

We staggered back into our life. The first day back in Brooklyn, I flinched every time the doorbell rang, thinking it would be the police with a warrant for the theft of the car. Max spent an hour on the phone with her sister, sitting in the hall chair with her face in her hands, and when it was over she said, "Inez is going to talk to Amma about the car."

"To drop the charges?"

"If any were filed. Inez said she's probably happy to let the whole thing go if she thinks it will make Aloysius unhappy."

I breathed easier. I took the Q train to my office in Union Square, stared at the papers on my desk for a while, and then went home and spent an afternoon pulling weeds out of our backyard. We both had the feeling you get as a child when you step off a merry-go-round—the spinning doesn't stop right away.

On Friday morning, Nick called and said, "Have you seen the *Times* today?"

"It's still out on the stoop," I said.

"Take a look at B35," he said.

Max was asleep upstairs. She had closed the bar the night before. I padded through the quiet house and took the paper in. At the back of the national section, I found this:

DIVORCE FILINGS ALLEGE MISMANAGEMENT, FRAUD AT COMSTOCK ESTATE

Max's mother had hired a blue-chip firm out of San Diego and was pursuing the divorce with the vigor of a Borgia. Her lawyers alleged, among other things, that an Australian national named Victor Griggs, sometimes known as St. James Albright, had swindled Aloysius Comstock out of $2.2 million with plans to build an agricultural research center. The money had gone to contracts and consultations that could not now be traced or verified, and Griggs had disappeared. Max's mother was petitioning for a freeze on all assets until they could be legally apportioned in the divorce. Nick and another reporter had the byline.

I called Nick back. "Well," I said.

"I've had a colleague out there keeping an eye on the new filings at the Los Angeles County courthouse," he said.

"You're welcome," I said.

"It's not a bad story," Nick said. "I hope Max won't be upset."

"Victor Griggs," I said.

"Are you surprised?"

"Not in the slightest," I said.

When Max came downstairs, I showed it to her. She laughed. "Well," she said. "What did I say?"

"You were right," I said.

"Anyone with eyes could see," she said.

"Two point two million."

She waved her hand. "That won't hurt him."

"Really?"

"I don't think so. Well, I don't know. Depends what he's got liquid."

I understood we were talking about Aloysius, although we would not use his name. She said, "As long as he's got his stake in the company, nothing touches him."

"It's a shame," I said.

"I'd rather he have it so Amma can take it," she said. She poured herself coffee, scraped jam over toast. I sat looking at the article upside down.

"What will Callisto do?" I said. "And all those other people who were hanging around?"

"I'm sure they'll vanish now that the spigot is being turned off."

"What would you have done with it, if you'd stayed there?" I said.

"What, the money?"

"Yeah," I said. "If you'd inherited your piece. Come into your trust."

"Well, those are two different things. A trust is a trickle. An inheritance is more like a bomb going off."

"Did you ever think about it?"

"Growing up?" she said. "I don't know. It's like Prince Charles, isn't it? I'm sure he wants to be king. But that means his mother has to die." She leaned on her elbows. "I don't think I thought of it as money, exactly. It just meant growing up.

Being in charge, finally. Except that I knew I would have to get married, so really it would be my husband in charge. Maybe that's why I didn't like to think about it."

"Hm," I said.

"Vera, come on," she said. "Tell me. I know you're thinking about it."

"Thinking about what?"

"What would *you* do with it?" she said. "That's what this is, when you ask. You're thinking what you would do with it."

I pulled back, exposed. "I guess I am."

"So?"

"Well, I would fix—"

"Of course, of course. You would fix everything that needs fixing around the house. And the car. And you'd get your bridge done and on and on. After all that."

"I'd buy a farm upstate for the summers," I said, "so we could run it into the ground. We could be the world's worst gentlemen farmers together."

"You want a farm?"

"I'd buy you a piano. I'd buy you six pianos. And then I'd give the rest of it away."

"Six pianos?"

"Do you want seven?"

"I'll take as many as you'll give me." She came and sat on my lap.

"Maybe you should meet my mother," I said.

The sun was coming in the window, which I had opened a crack to the cool air of the backyard. It was forecast to be another beautiful May day. From outside I could hear buses on Bedford Avenue, the starling that nested under the eaves of our shed, a telephone ringing in a neighbor's house. I had not thought this through. It seemed right that it should merely tumble out, that I shouldn't consider it too hard, and that I should feel a brief pulse of abject fear now that I'd said it, looking up into her calm eyes.

"Of course," she said. "Anytime."

⊕

The 2:05 to Washington, DC, departed from track 13. I kept looking at my watch. We stood on the platform in the dank underground of Penn Station, our overnight bags at our feet.

"We don't even have to stay the night," I said, for the second time. "We can turn right back around if we want to."

"Arrive at five thirty, depart at seven?"

"If we want to."

"I can't imagine you doing anything so dramatic," Max said.

That was a fair point. "We'll just have dinner and go to bed. Our tickets are exchangeable. We can leave anytime tomorrow."

"Maybe she'll be lovely," Max said. "Maybe she'll be wild about me."

"Ah. Maybe," I said.

Max slept on the train. She could sleep in any position, with nothing to rest her head on but her hands. I sat staring at the pages of a paperback. After Philadelphia, I left her peacefully arranged in her seat and walked to the club car, bought a whiskey soda, drank it standing up in two minutes, and then picked my way back to my seat, feeling distinctly worse.

The commuter towns of the Northeast Corridor rolled past. It had been some time—two years, maybe—since I had last made this trip. I had gone alone that time, as every time before. My mother had not met me at the station, which I had expected. It was difficult to imagine her standing hopefully in the crowd on the platform, watching the train empty out. And she was working anyway. I had taken the bus from Union Station to Friendship Heights and then walked a long way to clear my head, arrived at the empty house, and let myself in with the key that was still concealed in some bric-a-brac in a flower bed next to the back steps. The house was more austere than I remembered it. My mother had arrived home an hour later and told me she was planning to sell it, although as far as I knew this plan had not advanced since then. She made spaghetti and we limited ourselves to talk about Lyndon Johnson. Before we went to bed she suggested, out of nowhere, that I could go to school for a teaching certificate.

"I'm not looking for work," I said. "I have a job."

"I don't even understand what you do," she said.

I was clearing the table. "Do you want to know?"

"You've explained it."

I had already told her that I did investigations. I had even, in what I could only much later admit might have been a bid to impress her, disclosed my time with the CIA, although not the specifics of what I did. She was a Washington woman through and through, and I thought government work would make sense to her. It didn't.

From there, it seemed we had little to say to each other on that visit. She never spoke Max's name, although we were living together already by then. She asked no questions about my work or my friends or my house in Brooklyn. I left before noon the next day.

⊕

Max woke up when we pulled into Union Station. I was reproaching myself already for having timed our arrival to the evening rush. I was agitated, knocking over both our bags into the aisle of the train. We stepped onto the platform in a river of passengers, and there was my mother. She was standing, preposterously, on a bench. I stopped and was immediately jostled forward. Max turned back and looked at me questioningly.

"That's her there," I said.

Elizabeth Kelly was dressed in a light raincoat, despite the warm day. Her hair was set in a permanent wave, as it had been time out of mind. She wore large wire-frame glasses and had on the trace of makeup that she considered appropriate, a guard against nakedness. Both hands were in her pockets. She looked out over the surging crowd impassively, as a shepherd looks out over a flock. It took some effort for us to cut our way through to her.

"Hello, Ma," I said.

"Oh, hello," she said, looking down from her height. "This train is always late."

"I didn't know you were coming to the station," I said.

"Hello," Max said, putting up her hand. It was like being introduced to a royal personage on a dais. "I'm Max. It's so good to meet you."

"How do you do," my mother said. They shook hands. How was it so effortless for my mother to show nothing at all in her face or gestures? Neither a smile nor the absence of one. Neither comfort nor discomfort.

"What in the world are you doing up there?" I said.

"Keeping an eye out for you," she said. "Help me down."

We got her down from the bench, and she led us to the stairs. Above, in the grand echoing hall, she headed purposefully for the street. "Did you drive?" I called after her.

"Good Lord, no," she said. "We'll take a cab."

In a taxi, she sat in the front while Max and I crowded into the back. She fell right away into a discussion with the driver about some scandal in the mayor's office, in which both of them seemed to be very well versed, although with slightly variant opinions. Max walked her fingertips along my leg, looking innocently out the window. This was something she did when she felt that I was letting my nerves get the best of me, and I adored and hated it in equal measure. I smacked her hand away, and she smothered a laugh. We crawled through traffic. My mother asked the driver if she could smoke. The windows were down, and the spring humidity of the Potomac rolled through the car, carrying exhaust fumes and flowering trees with it. I was always a child again in this place. We were passing a rental hall where my sixth-grade orchestra held a Christmas concert. Around the block was the department store where my mother always took me for new shoes, where a salesman would kneel and hold my foot against a metal scale. The restaurant where we had sundaes on the most special occasions; the building where my father worked when I was so young that he still carried me through the lobby to say hello to the girls at the front desk.

We reached Chevy Chase. It was a beautiful late afternoon in the green suburbs. The sound of lawn mowers came in through the open windows. A light veil of spring leaves was turning to the dense cover of proper summer, which started early here. "This one," my mother said, knocking on the dash and pointing. We pulled into the driveway. My mother paid the driver and went ahead of us into the house, calling back, "I ordered in dinner yesterday and put it up. We just have to heat it."

The house looked lightly occupied. My mother went through to the kitchen while Max and I stood in the hall, fitting our overnight bags into a coat closet. I heard the twanging old springs of the oven door, the *thunk* of a glass bottle being set on a counter—gin, most likely. "Do you girls want a drink?" she called.

"She seems friendly," Max whispered.

"Yes, thank you," I called back.

"'You girls,'" said Max. "That's friendly, I think."

"She's asking if lesbians drink gin and tonics," I said. Max swatted me.

My mother suggested eating outside, on the brick patio under the tulip poplar in back. This seemed very festive of her. I was beginning to wonder if Max was right, if she was signaling some general approval of us. I felt off-kilter. We went out, holding our sweating drinks, propping the screen door open with a ceramic frog so we could ferry out the dinner that had been ordered the day before, which turned out to be a roast with vegetables and mash, volcanically reheated. My mother carved. Max crossed her legs at the ankle and leaned toward her and asked her questions about her work. I had never noticed before how beautiful Max's table manners were. I could feel my mother noticing it too. I ate silently, too fast, and watched this performance. My mother was explaining something about a contract with a printer and how it was being renegotiated and how this was a nightmare that filtered down to the editing bullpen. I had a curious feeling of watching them from above. And then, for an instant, I found that I was addressing my father in my mind, saying, *Don't you like her?*

There was a carton of ice cream for dessert and a bottle of Hershey's chocolate syrup. Max had had two drinks and was pointing her toes. We cleared the dishes and went back into the house as dark fell. Max took our bags up to the spare bedroom— my old bedroom. I stacked dishes and ran water in the sink. My mother was packing the leftover food into bowls with fitted tops. The news was on the radio, as it always was.

"Well," I said, after a few minutes of the kind of silence that my mother could easily sustain for hours, "what do you think?"

"What do I think of what?" she said.

I turned from the sink, my hands dripping onto my skirt. "Of Max," I said.

"Oh." She was searching for something in a cabinet. "Well, I think she's very nice. Polite girl."

I went back to the dishes. I felt a knot between my shoulder blades. What was it that I wanted? After all this time—I was clenching my jaw. It was the idea that my mother could turn this event into a nonevent; that what I had risked by bringing Max here might be sifted and wafted into nothing by the simple tools of denial, by Liz Kelly refraining from acknowledging

218

that it had happened at all. I said, "We're together." I had not planned to say this. In my confusion I lost my grip on a plate and splashed soapy water all over my front.

"You're what?" said my mother.

I could only press forward. My heart was hammering. "She's my girlfriend."

She looked steadily at me. Then she turned away and said, "I don't know why you have to make your life difficult."

"I'm making it difficult?"

"You need to work," she said. "Do you ever think about your reputation?"

"I am working," I said. "I've always been working. What does my work have to do with any of it? My work is full of queers too, Ma."

She flinched from the word, as I had intended. Then she said, "I don't understand why you're always so angry with me."

"I'm not angry with you," I said, which of course was a lie.

She sat down. She set her elbows on the table among the bowls and plastic containers. We were quiet for a minute. I dried my hands. She said, "Was I right about Joanne?"

I laughed. On the radio they were reading the box scores. "Yeah, you were right about Joanne."

"You two were very close," she said.

"I wrote her crazy letters." I wrote them in juvenile detention, after my mother forbade me from seeing Joanne and had me arrested for stealing the car. I never sent them.

"I worried about it," she said.

"What do you want me to say, Ma?" I said. I had long since stopped litigating the incident in my mind. It was no longer possible to imagine a version of my life in which it hadn't happened—in which my mother and I had never fought and I had never taken the car to Baltimore, never been adjudicated. Never sent away. To remove that one thread would unravel much of my life.

"I don't know." She had both hands flat on the table. She was looking at her rings. "I was on my own. Other women talk about their instincts. Other mothers. I never felt I had instincts. I was always trying to guess the right thing to do. And when I was a girl, you know—I mean, I would have been beaten within an inch of my life. No one would have thought twice."

I remembered this refrain from childhood arguments, and I was not interested in it.

"It was a long time ago, Ma," I said.

"I just wanted you to be happy," she said. "I wanted you to have a good life."

I stared at her. "I do," I said. "I am. That's what I'm trying to tell you."

I could see plainly in her face that this possibility had not occurred to her. She sat and let it work its way through her mind. I felt all at once that our misunderstanding was very simple, and it centered on this point. I wanted to laugh. "I came all this way to tell you that," I said. "I wanted you to know."

⊕

Each year we went on the Fourth of July to Riis Beach, where the various queer constituencies of New York came to rest and sunbathe and gossip, to see and be seen. Police cars occasionally cruised at half speed down Rockaway Beach Boulevard, but they never stopped, and an odd feeling of invincibility, of great numbers and therefore great strength casually and beautifully displayed, hung in the bright air over the beach. On this particular Fourth, we arrived early with our friends in a caravan of cars, hauling baskets and coolers across the sand, iced tea and gin lemonades, stacks of sandwiches that Peach and Sylvia had made. Nick wobbled in sandals with quarts of macaroni salad and cut watermelon, and there were two more girls from the bar that Max had invited, and roommates and girlfriends and somebody's cousins from Connecticut. We chose a place not far from the old bathhouses to spread out our many blankets, wrestled our umbrellas into the sand, and creaked open our beach chairs. Sylvia set up her radio. Nick and a friend unfurled a volleyball net, while Peach shouted at them that no one was planning to exert themselves in any way, and they could save themselves the trouble. She had removed her top already, which she referred to as bathing *à la française.* The beach around us was filled with what, to my eyes, seemed like kids: many topless, accompanied by their own radios, wearing the kind of sunglasses that sold for fifty cents on the racks on St. Marks Place, lying on picnic blankets loosely draped in each other's arms. I tugged on Max's arm and we went for a walk together along the edge of the water, foam washing over our ankles. White and lavender oysters the size of fingernails dug themselves frantically into the sand in the wash that followed each wave. We walked until the scrum on the sand had thinned out, until we were facing an uncertain stretch of beach half-screened by plastic fencing and backed by apartment blocks, and then circled slowly back.

By the time the fireworks began that night, we were back home, on our own roof, sunburned and tired, having just washed the salt and sand out of our hair. We sat in folding chairs beside the defunct chimney, eating a meal out of boxes from a West Indian takeout counter on Flatbush Avenue.

The big fireworks came from boats in the river. Small, unsanctioned displays stippled the sky to the south, popping in fits and starts deep into Brooklyn. We were quiet. Gold and silver crackled in the black sky, showers of red and blue. An ice cream truck circled our block, its song fading toward Nostrand Avenue, and then made another hopeful pass. There was money to be made this Sunday night, even though the children were in bed. Groups of revelers were out, liberated by the holiday.

Sunset had cooled the air only a little. The breeze against our skin was as warm as a breath.

"We're on an island up here, aren't we?" said Max.

"Oh, no," I said. "We're in the top of a tree. Do you know, when I moved in here, there was a nest in the chimney?"

She laughed. "Well, that's all right," she said. "A tree is more sociable."

We stretched our legs, crossed our ankles. There was nothing we needed to say. Charcoal smoke drifted out to us from Prospect Park. There was a lot of summer left, and after that, the rich, bright fall. Winter was for other people. We would sleep soon and sleep well.

ACKNOWLEDGMENTS

My most heartfelt thanks to Masie Cochran, my collaborator and guide in this project; Soumeya Bendimerad Roberts, for her advocacy and friendship; Jakob Vala and Diane Chonette, for their impeccable design; Nanci McCloskey, Becky Kraemer, Alex Gonzales, and Sangi Lama for their tireless and innovative support of their titles; Elizabeth DeMeo and Alyssa Ogi, for their sensibility and style; and of course Win McCormack and Craig Popelars, for what they have built and are building.

Thanks to Mark, first, last and always, who made it possible every day for me to sit down and work, and who brought our toddler down the hall to deliver an egg on toast and a cup of coffee so many mornings.

A COVID note: writing this book kept me from losing my mind entirely during the first year of the pandemic. So, my sincere thanks to this book.

READER'S GUIDE

1. How would you describe Vera's relationship with Max? What do you think draws Vera to Max, and vice versa?

2. Were you surprised by the luxury of the Comstock Estate? How do you think this environment influenced Max growing up, and shaped the person she is today?

3. Who, in your mind, is the villain of this novel? Could there be more than one?

4. What did you learn about the historical attitudes of the time period? Was there anything that caught you off guard?

5. Do you consider this a "road trip novel"? How does the passing landscape play a role?

6. This is the most personal case Vera Kelly has worked. How did her relationship with Max help or hinder the investigation?

7. If you've read all the books, in what ways has Vera changed from *Vera Kelly Is Not a Mystery* and *Who Is Vera Kelly?* Are there ways in which she has stayed the same?

8. Vera Kelly's group meeting at the Mineral Springs Hospital is a turning point of the book. Do you think the author's background as a licensed therapist informs this scene?

9. What did you think of Vera's visit with her mother at book's end? How does backstory from earlier books come into play?

10. What do you think the future holds for Vera Kelly?

ROSALIE KNECHT is the author of *Who Is Vera Kelly?*; *Vera Kelly Is Not a Mystery*, winner of the Edgar Award / G.P. Putnam's Sons Sue Grafton Memorial Award and a finalist for a Lambda Literary Award; as well as *Relief Map*; and a translation of César Aira's *The Seamstress and the Wind*. She lives in Jersey City, New Jersey.

DON'T MISS THE FIRST TWO BOOKS IN THE VERA KELLY SERIES

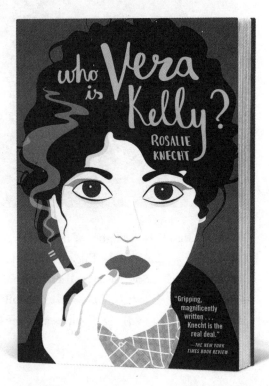

"Gripping, magnificently written . . . Knecht is the real deal."
—*THE NEW YORK TIMES BOOK REVIEW*

2021 EDGAR AWARD, G.P. PUTNAM'S SONS SUE GRAFTON MEMORIAL AWARD WINNER

LAMBDA LITERARY AWARDS FINALIST

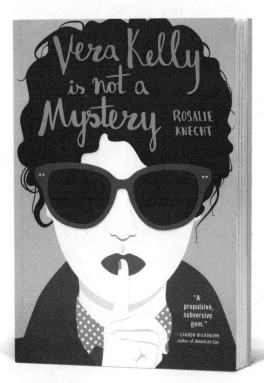

"A propulsive, subversive gem."
—LAUREN WILKINSON, author of *American Spy*